ELLA AT EDEN

To Steph and Nathan—for the bell tower.

First American Edition 2021
Kane Miller, A Division of EDC Publishing

Text copyright © Laura Sieveking, 2020.
Cover and internal illustrations copyright © Scholastic Australia, 2020.
Cover and internal illustrations by Danielle McDonald.
Design by Keisha Galbraith.
Laura Sieveking asserts her moral rights as the author of this work.
Danielle McDonald asserts her moral rights as the illustrator of this work.

First published by Scholastic Australia, an imprint of Scholastic Australia Pty Limited.
This edition published under license from Scholastic Australia Pty Limited.

For information contact:
Kane Miller, A Division of EDC Publishing
5402 S. 122nd E. Ave, Tulsa, OK 74146
www.kanemiller.com
www.myubam.com

Library of Congress Control Number: 2021930851

Printed and bound in the United States of America

1 2 3 4 5 6 7 8 9 10

ISBN: 978-1-68464-358-5

EDEN
COLLEGE

ELLA AT EDEN

The Secret Journal

LAURA SIEVEKING

Kane Miller
A DIVISION OF EDC PUBLISHING

Eden College

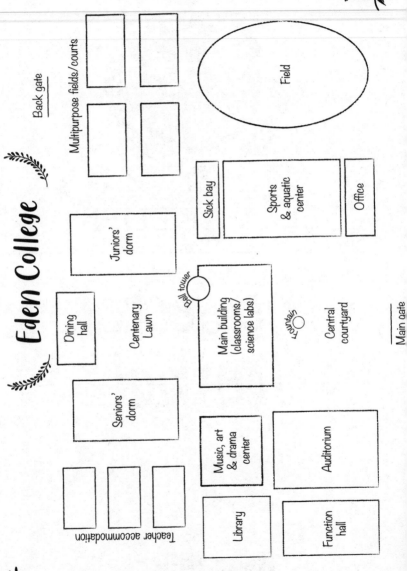

Multipurpose fields/courts

Back gate

Field

Juniors' dorm

Sick bay

Sports & aquatic center

Office

Dining hall

Centenary Lawn

Bell tower

Main building (classrooms/ science labs)

Fountain

Central courtyard

Main gate

Seniors' dorm

Music, art & drama center

Auditorium

Teacher accommodation

Library

Function hall

4

Juniors' Dorm

Year 7 rooms

Level 2

7	Bathroom
8	
9	
10	
11	
12	

6	
5	
4 Ella's room	
3	
2	
1	

Level 1 (ground)

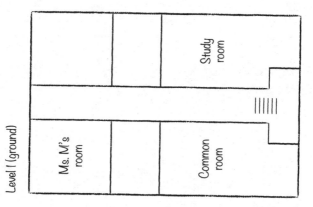

Ms. M's room

Study room

Common room

Chapter 1

The sun shone down, seeping through my panama hat and into my chestnut-brown hair. I could hear a lorikeet chattering in the distance as a warm summer breeze rustled through the slightly parched leaves of the distant bush trees. I walked along the path, which snaked its way around the central courtyard, gently running my hand across the manicured hedge that hugged its edge.

As I passed the main building of classrooms, I saw Violet walking ahead of me. I knew it was her as soon as she glanced up at the tree beside her. Her profile showed her pale face shining in the sunlight, with rays bouncing off her round glasses. She looked out of place walking around a high school campus because she was so little. Sometimes I'd catch myself thinking she was my little sister, Olivia.

"Violet!" I called out.

She spun around and smiled at me. I jogged to catch up with her.

"How's it going?" I asked.

"Pretty good," she said, linking arms with me.

I couldn't believe how different Violet was from when I first met her. Early on, Violet seemed completely reclusive (that means someone who doesn't like socializing with other people). But then I found out that Violet wasn't really like that at all. She was just really nervous everyone would find out about her diabetes and judge her for being different. Since she admitted to us that she has diabetes, it's like a weight has been lifted off her shoulders. She's been hanging out with me, Zoe and Grace a lot. This is pretty cool because we are all in the same dorm room.

We walked across Centenary Lawn and through to the dining hall. Inside, girls were bustling about collecting their afternoon tea. Some sat at the long benches and tables inside, while others took their food outside to the lawn.

I looked in the baskets set out on one of the tables. There were apples and bananas, and some kind of oatmeal bar. It looked delicious. I grabbed an apple and an oatmeal bar.

"I'm just going to the kitchen to get my food," Violet said. Having diabetes meant Violet needed to stick to a particular diet, so her food was specially prepared by the chef.

"I'll wait for you," I smiled.

Violet skipped into the kitchen.

"If you have your food, please either move to a table or go outside," an irritated voice bellowed over the chatter. It was Ms. Montgomery. Ms. Montgomery is the Vice Headmistress of the school and also the Juniors' Housemistress. Her eyebrows were furrowed and her eyes darted from left to right as she took in the chaos

9

of afternoon tea. It clearly bothered her. She looked at us all like we were a swarm of ants crawling over her coffee table.

Violet came back out of the kitchen with her food and we hurried past Ms. Montgomery.

"Walking, please," she scolded.

We immediately slowed to a leisurely stroll, but then accelerated into a run as soon as we'd cleared the dining hall doors, away from her watchful eyes. We giggled as we ran over to one of the big trees that grew on the side of the lawn. Underneath, Grace and Zoe were already sitting down in the dappled sunlight.

"Took your time," Grace scoffed, as we collapsed next to them.

"Monty said to *walk*," Violet said sternly, imitating Ms. Montgomery's serious face.

We all laughed.

I looked around at my little group. Violet with her pale skin and glasses glinting in the sunlight. Zoe with her Italian olive skin and dark bob. And Grace with her hair in a long, dark braid and effervescent (that means bright and sparkly) cat-green eyes.

My Nanna Kate says that friendship groups need balance, like a good cake recipe. Not too much sugar or too much salt. Just the right amount of everything. Grace was proving to be our "sugar"—the hit of humor and mischief we all needed, especially when we were feeling down. Violet had a quietness about her and was an amazing listener. She never jumped in and told you what you were feeling—she always quietly helped you work it out for yourself. And Zoe—my BFF since we were five. So smart, logical and wise.

And where did I fit? I think I'm a person who feels things pretty deeply. Mum thinks I can be too dramatic, but my Nanna Kate says I am "emotionally intuitive." She says that means I can tell what people are feeling and I understand. Nanna Kate says this is a good thing, but it also means I need to be careful not to make decisions with my heart over my head every time.

"So, who's excited about tomorrow's field trip?" Grace asked.

"It's so weird," Zoe mused. "I only thought about it

the other day, but this will be our first time being more than five minutes away from school since we started here!"

I frowned. Zoe was right. Living at school meant almost all our days were spent on campus. On the weekend, we were allowed to walk to the local shops with the Senior girls to get ourselves a treat, but, other than that, we rarely went anywhere. Of course, there would be holidays and exeats (that's weekends where we go home for a visit), but, on the whole, we were always at Eden College.

This didn't bother me as much as I thought it would. Eden had everything I could ever want. We were allowed to use the school pool on hot afternoons and weekends. We could use the tennis courts or the field for playing games or sports, and the music, art and drama center if we felt like being crafty. Our dormitory was pretty cool, too—we had a big TV and a huge common room to hang out with our friends in.

Life was pretty good at Eden. The only thing really missing was my family. The thought of Max and

Olivia and Mum and Dad sprung up on me like an unwelcome fright. I startled, then took a deep breath. Homesickness was something we were always going to have to deal with while we lived at school.

"Ella?" Zoe asked, breaking my train of thought.

"Oh, sorry, what was that?"

"Are you excited about the field trip tomorrow?" Zoe repeated.

"Yeah, it'll be good," I said, nodding. "I have to start thinking about some new articles for *Eden Press*, and I figured the field trip might give me some ideas."

I had just been made Junior Journalist for our online school newspaper. This meant I was responsible for coming up with stories particularly relevant to the Juniors in Year 7.

"Zoe, can I be your bus buddy?" Grace blurted.

"Sure," Zoe smiled.

Something in my chest lurched. *It's fine*, I thought to myself.

"Ella, will you sit with me?" Violet asked.

I smiled and nodded. I had to remember I was in high

school now. And that meant Zoe and I would be making new friendships. It wasn't like primary school anymore. But the thought of Zoe and Grace together on the bus tugged at my heart just a little.

"So, what should I write about the field trip tomorrow? For *Eden Press*, I mean," I said, after swallowing a mouthful of afternoon snack. "How cool would it be if we discovered something at the museum!"

Grace waved her arm dismissively. "Oh, Ella, you know what happens on these trips. We ride in a bus, we get there, we walk around with some old guide who points out old things, we eat, we get back on the bus and someone pukes. End of story."

Zoe laughed loudly.

I frowned. "It's not like that, Grace. What if something exciting happens? What if there's a robbery or we crack an ancient Egyptian code?"

"As if," Grace laughed.

I picked up a sweet-gum pod from the ground and gently threw it at Grace in mock irritation.

"Hey!" she protested. "Those spiky suckers hurt!"

She picked up one of the spiky pods from behind her and lobbed it back at me. But it sailed over my head and hit something behind me.

"Ow! What gives?"

We turned around to see Saskia rubbing her arm angrily as she walked past with her friends, Portia and Mercedes.

"Oops!" Grace whispered. Then she yelled, "It was Ella!"

"Hey! Was not!" I exclaimed, indignant. "Grace is lying!"

Saskia frowned at me and wrinkled up her nose as she walked away.

Grace laughed heartily.

"Grace! Saskia already has problems with me. Don't make it worse," I said. But I couldn't help smiling just a bit.

Saskia was the school diva. She loved being the best at everything, and loved drama even more. Not Drama as in the subject. I love that kind of Drama. No, I mean drama as in fights and scandals and getting everyone into trouble. I thought we had come to a bit of an understanding when I kept a secret for her recently. But even after that, she still seemed so volatile. That means unpredictable.

Violet dusted off her dress and Grace stood up and took a basketball shot at the trash can with her apple core. It bounced slightly off the rim of the can, then clunked inside.

"Yes!" Grace celebrated.

"What are you all doing now?" Violet asked.

"Computer for homework," Zoe sighed.

"Me, too," said Grace.

"I've got orchestra rehearsal, but I need to grab my flute from the dorm," I said.

"I'll come with you, Ella," Violet said. "I need to get changed for ballet."

We all began walking toward the dormitory, which was across the other side of Centenary Lawn. As we approached the house, Grace linked arms with Zoe and pulled her ahead.

"Let's go, Zo!" she yelled. Zoe laughed loudly and

skipped into the house with Grace. I stopped where I was and watched as the front door shut behind them.

"You OK, Ella?" Violet asked, as she opened the door in front of me.

"Yeah, fine," I said, shaking my head just a little.

"Come on, then!" she giggled.

I grabbed the door from Violet as she walked inside. Glancing toward the study room, I gently lifted my hand to my chest, then let it drop. I hurried up the stairs after Violet to get my flute for orchestra rehearsal.

Chapter 2

X   —

From: <u>Ella</u>

Sent: Monday, 5:05 PM

To: <u>Olivia</u>

Subject: **Going out!**

Hi Olivia!

How are you? Why didn't you email me last week?? Too busy practicing your part for the school musical, I bet. How's that all going? Has Matilda gotten over her stage fright yet? I bet you'll be a good friend and help her like you always do.

Speaking of friends . . . things here are great. Violet, me, Grace and Zoe are all getting along really well. I'm so lucky to have such great room buddies. But . . . I dunno. It's kinda different than primary school. Like, people don't have BFFs here—you're meant to kinda have a group. Zoe is still my best friend, I think. But sometimes . . . I dunno. Ignore me, I'm just being a baby.

Tomorrow we are getting out of this place! Haha! Sounds like I live in jail. It's exciting though—we are going to the museum for the day. It's going to be totally fun. Mr. Quinn (my history teacher) said we might even be able to get ice cream at the end of the day if we are all super-duper well-behaved. But Monty (Ms. Montgomery, remember?) had a big frown when he said that, so we'll have to wait and see if it actually happens. She is SUCH a fun-police.

Email me ASAP.

Miss you!

Love, Ella

xx

The bus pulled out of the front gate of Eden College and gathered speed as it chugged up the road. The long private driveway was lined with tall green trees, which were full and round with the cloak of summer. Through the open window, cicadas chirped and kookaburras cackled.

But the sounds of wildlife were quickly replaced with the chatter of excited 11- and 12-year-old girls, eager to go on an outing. I watched as my school disappeared behind me. I could see the ornate turrets of the main building, and the big bronzed bell sat silently in the bell tower, like an old retired relative, happy to watch without speaking himself.

I'd only been at Eden a short time, but much of it already felt like home. Even though I missed my family and my real home every day, I'd noticed how parts of Eden were being etched into my mind and heart, like the freckle on my hand or the birthmark on my thigh.

I looked at Violet sitting beside me and smiled. "You feeling OK, Violet?" I checked. Now that I knew Violet had diabetes, I liked to make sure she was OK. I think she mostly appreciated that we were all looking out for her, but sometimes she rolled her eyes at me like I was a nagging mum.

"You asked me that already," she laughed. "And yes, I'm fine."

Grace spun around in the seat in front of us. "Right, time to make this more fun."

Zoe raised her eyebrows.

"Who wants to do a dare?" Grace asked excitedly, as she jittered in her seat.

"No way, I'm OUT," I moaned. "Remember what happened last time we played Truth or Dare? I had to pretend to sleepwalk to save you all from getting into massive trouble with Monty. Uh-uh."

Grace looked hopefully from Zoe to Violet. Both girls looked at each other, then rolled their eyes and shook their heads.

"Oh, you boring people!" Grace said, throwing her hands up.

"What's on offer?" a voice asked from across the aisle of the bus.

Saskia.

Grace smiled, sensing prey. "Well," she said slowly. "I'll challenge you to a dare on the field trip. If you do it and succeed, I have to accept whatever dare you throw me back at school. Deal?"

Saskia's eyes glittered. "Deal," she purred.

Grace turned back to us, clapping her hands together with glee.

"Grace, don't you ever learn?" Zoe scolded, play-punching Grace in the arm. "NEVER make a deal with Saskia."

"Oh, she's fine. Her bark is worse than her bite," Grace giggled.

"What are you going to dare her to do?" Violet asked.

"I don't know yet. But it will come to me. Just wait till we get there."

Grace bounced around excitedly in her seat for the rest of the journey, chattering away to Zoe next to her. I got my notebook out of my bag and flicked it open. I'd written down a few ideas for my next big story for *Eden Press*. I definitely wanted to do something inspired by the field trip, but I wasn't exactly sure what yet. I didn't want to just do a boring article recounting our day walking around. I needed something *more*.

The bus ambled on, until we finally pulled up outside a grand old building in the middle of the city. The sandstone construction had an ornate frontage and a big sign saying "National Museum" hung across the front. Everyone began to rustle around in their seats, gathering their bags and hats and trying to stand up.

"Girls, sit down!" a stern voice cut across the chatter. Ms. Montgomery frowned and waved for us all to be seated and quiet.

"Put on your panama hats and keep them on your heads for the duration of the field trip," she said. "Now, I needn't remind you that Eden Girls are always on their best behavior in public. While you are walking around in the museum, you will be representing your school. So I want no foolish or disrespectful behavior." Her beady eyes darted around the bus, accusingly. "You will now *quietly* stand and file out of the bus in an orderly fashion."

We all filed off the bus, thanking the driver on our way out. I squinted in the sunshine and pulled my panama hat down, but it didn't stop the bright sunlight from bouncing off the sidewalk, making me wince. We walked inside the museum and gathered quietly in the foyer, while Ms. Montgomery and Mr. Quinn sorted out our tickets at the front counter.

They came back from the desk and broke us into smaller groups. Luckily, they did this simply by bundling us into groups of about ten with the people standing closest to us. This meant Violet, Grace, Zoe and I were all in the same group, much to our surprise and delight. Our group also consisted of Saskia and her two friends, Portia and Mercedes, as well as Annabelle and Ruby.

"Perfect," Saskia purred. "I'm ready for my dare, Grace."

Grace smiled mischievously.

"Each group will be allocated a museum guide, who will take them around the exhibits. I trust you will be respectful toward your guide and will listen carefully.

Any bad reports from the guides will result in loss of privileges back at school," Ms. Montgomery said sternly.

The museum staff each walked up to a different group and introduced themselves. I looked at the group to my left, who had been allocated a young guy with dreadlocks in his hair.

"Are you ready for an adventure?" he yelled. All the girls nodded eagerly. "I can't hear you!" he cried.

"YEAH!" they cheered, as Ms. Montgomery shook her head disapprovingly.

"Let's go, explorers!" the guy shouted, waving for his group of girls to follow him.

I couldn't help but smile, too. Maybe this trip was going to be—

"Right, are we ready?" a stern voice said.

We looked at each other, confused. Ms. Montgomery stood in front of us.

"Where's our guide?" Saskia asked.

"There aren't enough museum staff to have one guide per group, so *I* am your guide," she answered flatly. "Mr. Quinn is taking one of the other groups, too."

We all stared.

"Well, stop gawking and let's get moving!" she said. Ms. Montgomery briskly walked off as we scrambled to follow her.

"Just our luck to get Monty as our guide!" Grace hissed.

We all nodded as we saw the group ahead skipping off with the cool guy with dreadlocks.

The groups all started in different parts of the museum. Our group was starting in the "Ancient Egypt" exhibit. There was a display recreating the Boy Pharaoh Tutankhamun's tomb, with all its amazing riches. It was so shiny and lavish (which means fancy and expensive-looking). We also saw some recreated masks from the pharaohs and their painted coffins. Then we watched a video about mummification, which Zoe thought was amazing but I thought was yuck, yuck, YUCK!

As we headed into the next exhibit, Grace gathered us all together.

"OK, Saskia, here's your dare," she whispered, careful not to catch Ms. Montgomery's attention.

"You have to hide in one of the display scenes in the next room without Monty catching you!"

"Grace, that's impossible," Portia protested. "Saskia is in uniform. Don't you think Monty will notice if there's an Eden Girl in a panama hat in the middle of a caveman scene?"

Saskia shushed her friend. "Challenge accepted," she chirped, putting out her hand for Grace to shake. "But remember, if I manage to do this dare without getting caught, you have to accept *my* dare for you back at school."

Grace shook Saskia's hand.

"Hurry up, girls!" Ms. Montgomery called.

We trotted into the next room, eager to see where Saskia would have to hide. There were huge model ships, as well as many different shiny artifacts (that means really old and valuable stuff from history).

"Vikings," Violet whispered.

"Grace, go distract Monty and let me get to work," Saskia whispered, as she disappeared among the displays.

"Where are all the helmets with horns?" Grace asked loudly.

"You'll find that is a common misconception," Ms. Montgomery answered. "Come over here, girls, and read the truth about Vikings. They were actually a very refined people, contrary to popular opinion these days. Look! Here are some artifacts from the time, including weapons, jewelry and other household items."

We all gathered around, looking at the Viking relics in the glass case.

I peeked behind me and saw that Saskia had completely disappeared.

We walked through the room, taking notes in our notebooks in case anything from the tour showed up on our history test. Right before the exhibit's exit, there was one final display.

"Look at this!" Ms. Montgomery breathed. It was a huge Viking ship with mannequins on board, dressed for war. "This isn't a real Viking ship," Ms. Montgomery continued. "It's simply a recreation of what historians think this kind of ship might have looked like. And see the outfits they are wearing? That shows us the climate was cold."

I looked at the scene in front of me. Suddenly, Grace burst out laughing.

"What is so funny?" Ms. Montgomery scolded.

"Oh, nothing," said Grace, smothering her giggles. "Just something I remembered from a movie I saw once. Maybe we should move on."

Ms. Montgomery frowned and nodded, leading the rest of the girls out of the room. As we turned to follow, Grace pointed back at the display, her hand over her mouth. There, in the middle of the Viking warriors, was a smaller Viking with shining blue eyes and glistening blond hair. She had a brown piece of sackcloth thrown over her and was frozen in a pose, pointing out to sea.

Saskia.

We all burst out laughing, and hurried into the next room so Monty wouldn't come back and see Saskia in the display.

It looked like Saskia had won the first round of dares after all!

Chapter 3

We continued through the museum, working our way up through time. I scribbled down notes in my notebook, not only in case we were tested at the end, but also in case I found a good story for *Eden Press*. I desperately hoped we'd foil a museum robbery because that would make a great story for the online newspaper. But everything seemed to be going disappointingly smoothly.

Toward the end of the visit, we found ourselves in the wartime exhibit. There was information about both World War I and II, which was interesting because we had been studying World War II in history class.

We walked around the room in a somber silence. *Somber* means deeply serious, or even a bit sad. I think it was because when you walk around the ancient rooms, like ancient Egypt or ancient Greece, it seems like such a faraway time—like you are stepping into a fairy story of talking cats and snake-headed monsters. But the war rooms didn't seem all that distant. There were photographs of children—not that different than us—sitting in classrooms during wartime. I couldn't imagine what that would have been like.

I quietly walked up to a display and read the information board. It was all about a woman in the country of Germany who helped children to escape from the enemy through secret underground tunnels. I shivered slightly.

Next to it was information about a secret diary that a young girl wrote during World War II. It told how she kept herself safe by hiding from the enemy in an attic. I frowned as I read it. I used to keep a diary, just like she did.

"What are you thinking, Ella?" a voice said from behind me.

I turned to see Ms. Montgomery looking gently at the display in front of us. She didn't have her characteristic frown on her face. The creases on her forehead had smoothed and her mouth was relaxed instead of pursed. Her voice was softer.

"I'm not sure," I said slowly. "I think I'm just imagining what it must have been like to be alive at that time."

Ms. Montgomery nodded. "It's really not all that long ago, you know. My grandparents were both children during the war."

"I think sometimes you forget that these were real people. Kids, just like us," I said.

Ms. Montgomery patted me on the shoulder and smiled ever so slightly. "That's an interesting thing to think about, wouldn't you say? Perhaps something interesting to *write* about, too."

I looked up into her eyes, perplexed. She shook her head lightly and frowned. "I'd better gather everyone together," she said, as she turned to walk away.

To write about, I thought. Could this be the article I needed for *Eden Press*?

I leaned in closer to a real photograph of a classroom. The children in the grainy black-and-white picture were practicing evacuating their classroom in a drill. They looked different than us, with their old-fashioned uniforms and haircuts. But when I looked at their faces, I saw ordinary kids. Just like me.

"Come on, Ella," Violet called, as she walked out of the war room. "Time for lunch!"

I took one last lingering look at the faded black-and-white photos of the classrooms and tunnels and the child's diary.

Maybe, I mused.

We gathered outside in the museum courtyard and the bus driver unloaded a cooler, which was filled with food from the Eden kitchen. We all selected a sandwich of our choice and a piece of fruit and took them with us as we found a shady spot to eat.

Grace, Zoe, Violet and I sat on the ground, as the

warmth from the pavement seeped through our light summer dresses.

"Can we join?"

I looked up and saw Saskia standing with Portia and Mercedes—they were never too far from her side.

Grace nodded and opened up our circle a little more.

"So, did I complete your dare satisfactorily?" Saskia asked.

"That was hilarious!" Grace laughed. "When Monty looked up at the Viking ship, I thought you were a goner. But you were so still!"

We all laughed at the memory of Saskia in the scene on the Viking ship.

"So, what's my dare?" Grace asked.

"I've thought of something," Saskia said, narrowing her eyes.

Mercedes and Portia let out little giggles. They clearly already knew Saskia's plans.

"Meet me at the back of the main building at school, tomorrow morning at sunrise," Saskia said. "And then I will give you your challenge."

"But we aren't allowed out of the dorms until breakfast," Violet said.

"You don't have to come!" Saskia sneered.

Violet's cheeks reddened.

"I'll be there," Grace said.

"Looking forward to it," Saskia smiled.

I had no idea what Saskia was going to challenge Grace to do, but I had a bad feeling about it.

Chapter 4

I looked out the window and saw the first rays of sunlight, glinting through the trees. A magpie warbled a tuneful morning song and a cockatoo squawked angrily into the fresh morning breeze. I turned around and saw Grace, who had thrown on light tracksuit pants and an old T-shirt. Zoe and Violet stood by her side.

"Are you sure you want to do this?" I asked. "This wouldn't be the first time we were in trouble for leaving our room out of hours."

Grace nodded firmly. "A dare's a dare, Ella. But you guys totally don't have to come. Honestly, I can handle

Saskia on my own."

"No way," said Zoe firmly. "We are friends, so we do this together."

Violet nodded nervously. She didn't seem as sure.

I followed the other three out of our room, checking the hallway for teachers or prefects. The inside of the boarding house was still dark with the remnants of night, the morning sunshine not yet beaming through the windows.

We crept silently up the carpeted hallway, being careful to walk right against the wall where the floorboards creaked less. When we got to the stairs, Grace went down by herself, just in case there was someone down there. It'd be easier to make up an excuse for being out of bed on her own. When she was confident the coast was clear, she waved to us at the top of the stairs. One by one we stalked down the winding staircase until we were all standing at the foot of it.

Suddenly, we heard movement behind us. Violet gasped, and I quickly clapped my hand over her mouth to stop her from screaming.

Meow.

Violet put her hand to her racing heart and shook her head. It was just Crystal—Ms. Montgomery's cat.

Grace gently unlocked the front door, which clicked open with a noisy *clack*. We all winced as it echoed down the hallway. I eyed Ms. Montgomery's bedroom door, which was at the back of the house. No movement.

Grace pushed open the front door, freezing every time it creaked. Finally, we bundled outside into the fresh morning air, quietly shutting the door behind us.

"Phase one complete," Grace breathed.

We all grabbed each others' hands and jogged across Centenary Lawn toward the back of the main building, where we had agreed to meet Saskia. As we jogged, our eyes darted from side to side, wary that the groundskeepers could already be around the school.

It didn't take us long to find Saskia standing by some rose bushes with Mercedes and Portia. She had a huge grin on her face and Portia and Mercedes looked like smug cats who had just caught mice.

"So, you came," Saskia grinned.

"Of course," Grace said, with her eyebrows raised. "So, what's the dare?"

Portia smothered a giggle.

"You have to climb to the top of the bell tower and ring the old bell," Saskia smiled.

"But the bell tower is out of bounds!" Violet said. "Nobody has been up there for years. And besides, the wooden door to the tower is always locked."

Saskia held out her hand. Dangling from it was an ancient-looking key.

"How'd you get that?" Zoe asked bluntly.

"I have my ways," Saskia said mysteriously.

Grace grabbed the old key from Saskia and turned to face the bell tower. A new expression crossed her face. She looked a little pale, and less confident than usual.

"Are you OK?" I whispered.

Grace began to walk over toward the bell tower door, but as she walked she pulled me in closer.

"This is probably not the time to admit this," she whispered, "but I am terrified of heights!"

"Don't do it then!" I hissed. "It's really high!"

"Well, I have to now, don't I?" she whispered back.

"Is there a problem?" Saskia called from behind us. "Because if you are chicken, just say so."

"Nup! I live for this stuff," Grace said loudly. But the wobble in her voice was unmistakable.

We all gathered around the old wooden door that led to the bell tower. Grace took the antique-looking key and pushed it into the lock. She turned it and it made a loud clunking noise. Once the door was unlocked, she handed the key back to Saskia, who slipped it into her pocket.

As Grace pulled the door open, a gust of air came rushing out of the stairwell. It was cold and dank and made us cough. We all peered inside. The stairwell was very dark—almost black—but we could make out a very narrow, winding staircase, which coiled upward as tight as a corkscrew.

Grace breathed in sharply.

"It . . . it might take me a while to get up there," she stammered. "It's pretty steep."

"OK, you go and we'll keep watch," Zoe said to Grace.

Grace took a tentative step forward. She put her foot on the first step and turned back to look at us.

"Too easy," she said. But the nerves in her voice betrayed her confidence.

As Grace ascended the staircase, she disappeared from view. We stood at the bottom of the bell tower, waiting.

It reminded me of the time my family went to an amusement park with my Nanna Kate. Max desperately wanted to go on the roller coaster with me and Olivia. When he was measured at the entry line, he was only just tall enough to get through—Dad joked that if it weren't for the hair gel spiking up his hair, he may not have made it. As we stood in the line, Olivia became more and more excited about the roller coaster. She's a complete daredevil. But Max became quieter and quieter.

As we neared the front of the line, the roller coaster seemed to grow taller and taller with every step we took. Max's eyes grew bigger and bigger, and his skin went all white. He looked like he wanted to be sick.

When we got to the front of the line, we saw Nanna Kate standing by the barrier. She leaned over and said, "Sometimes it takes more courage to say 'no' and face the embarrassment of backing out, than it does to do something you don't want to do."

We all stared at Max, as relief flooded over his face. He climbed up the bars of the barrier and Nanna Kate lifted him over. Then they went and got cotton candy.

I wished I'd remembered that story *before* Grace had started climbing the bell tower.

We waited for what seemed like forever.

"Look!" Violet said finally, pointing up to the top of the bell tower. "She's up there!"

We all stumbled back to get a better view. Just peeping over the ledge of the belfry, we could see a little hand waving.

Then a loud *GONG* sounded from the top of the tower.

"We'd better get out of here!" Portia squealed. "If the teachers hear that sound, they are going to know somebody is in the bell tower. Let's go!"

Saskia, Portia and Mercedes bolted away.

"Hurry up, Grace!" Zoe called.

We waited.

"Grace?" Violet yelled. She looked around nervously.

"You guys go," I said. "I'll wait for Grace. No point in all of us putting ourselves at risk."

Zoe and Violet looked at each other with worried eyes.

"Seriously, go!" I said.

Zoe and Violet nodded. "We'll cover for you," said Zoe, and they trotted away.

"Grace—you OK up there?" I yelled through my cupped hands.

No response.

Grace had been up there for ages and I began to worry. What if she'd hit her head on the bell? What if she'd fallen?

There was only one thing to do. I walked into the bell tower and began to climb. The stairway was incredibly tight and I could easily put a hand on each wall without even stretching my arms out. It was very dim and cold, and I began to feel a little dizzy as I walked around and around and around the corkscrewing stairwell. I glanced back down behind me, only to see darkness. My head swooned slightly.

I continued to wind my way upward, wondering if the staircase was ever going to end. Finally, I saw a glimmer of light, and I emerged into the small area where the huge bell lived at the top of the tower. It hung there, an old bronzed color, with a large crack down the middle. I looked past it and out across the school. The tower was so high! I could see over the dorm to the surrounding bushland.

But where was Grace?

I walked around the huge bell until I saw her, huddled with her knees tucked up to her chest, sitting on the cold stone floor.

"Are you OK?" I gasped, crouching down beside her. "Are you hurt?"

Grace's face was in her hands. She jerked her head up at the sound of my voice. "No, I'm not hurt. What are you doing up here?"

"I came to find you!"

"Sorry—I started to make my way back down the stairwell, but I just got really overwhelmed. It's so high up here and those stairs are so steep and I have such a bad fear of heights," she said, her voice shaky.

"Why didn't you call for help?"

Grace shrugged. "I didn't want Saskia thinking I was a chicken."

I put my arm around Grace. "Don't worry," I said soothingly. "We'll sit here for a bit till you feel better, then I will lead you back down. There are no teachers around yet, and we still have plenty of time before our wake-up call."

"Really?" Grace asked. She looked pale and small—nothing like the usual Grace.

We sat together in silence, listening to the morning songs of the surrounding bush birds. I think it was the first time I'd ever heard Grace be silent for a long period of time. She usually even talked in her sleep!

As I sat, looking around me, I began to run my fingers

along the stone wall we were leaning against. One of the stones was a bit loose and I fidgeted with it, wobbling it to and fro.

Suddenly, the stone brick fell right out of the wall.

"Are you breaking the bell tower?" Grace asked, laughing.

"No, I just . . ."

My voice trailed off. As I'd gone to put the brick back into the wall, I noticed there was something blocking it. I peered inside the space and saw something reddish brown. It looked like old leather. I reached my fingers in and tried to pry the item out of the wall.

"What have you found?" Grace asked, curious.

"I'm not sure," I said, as I continued to jimmy the item in the wall. After a few seconds, the thing came loose and spilled out onto the cold stone floor of the bell tower.

It was old.

It was weathered.

It was a book.

And on the front in faded gold letters was a word.
I dusted the dirt off the cover with my fingers to reveal
the writing.

DIARY

Chapter 5

From: <u>Ella</u>

Sent: Wednesday, 8:05 AM

To: <u>Olivia</u>

Subject: Discovery!

Hi Olivia,

I have to type quickly because classes start in half an

hour. I just found the most amazing thing! I had to

rescue Grace from the top of the bell tower (long story—

I'll tell you later), and I found something hidden in the

stone wall up there. Can you guess what it was? You'll never guess, so I'll just tell you.

It's a DIARY!

It's not like my diary that you used to try and steal from my bedroom. It's way older than that. I think it might be, like, 100 years old or something! The cover is really worn and it looks really old-fashioned.

I haven't had a chance to read it yet, but the writing inside looks like it's right out of the olden days. It's kinda curly and pretty and written in blotchy ink. I don't know who wrote it, or what it's about, but if someone took the time to hide it in a wall, then it must be very special and totes full of secrets!

I can't wait to read it! I'll tell you all about it soon.

Love, Ella

xx

I quickly slapped my laptop shut. We weren't meant to use our laptops in our bedrooms—we were only meant to use them for homework and only in the study room downstairs. But I just *had* to email Olivia as soon as possible.

I put my laptop on the small desk in our room and jumped back onto my bed. I still had time to have a quick look before class. I reached under my pillow, where I had put the diary for safekeeping, and gently pulled it out.

I turned it over in my hands. The burgundy leather was wearing off and tiny pieces flaked onto my lap. It looked like an ancient artifact from the museum. I was going to have to be extra careful with this book.

I gently opened the diary to find that the pages inside were yellow and weathered. They felt crunchy and dry between my fingers as I carefully leafed through the first few pages.

In beautiful, black inky letters that swirled at the ends were the words:

Diary of Elena

"Elena," I whispered to myself. I wondered who she was. And why she had hidden her diary.

I turned to the first entry.

1940?! That was AGES ago! I couldn't believe my eyes. It wasn't quite 100 years old like I'd imagined, but it wasn't that far off either!

I continued to read.

My first entry in my very own diary. Papa sent it to me for my twelfth birthday, just this week! It was very kind of him. I know what a privilege it is to own such a handsome, leather-bound book of my very own.

But what does one write in such a beautiful book? Mama said I should keep a record of my learnings. Papa said I should write essays to make sure my English is perfect. That way I am not wasting all those years of English tutoring I had when we lived in Italy. Nonna said I should write the words of my heart—I think I like her idea most of all. But even though Italian is my heart's language, I will continue to write in English, to please Papa.

I have only been a student at Eden College for a short time. Papa says I must do my very best to gain an exemplary education. He says he did not move us across the seas to simply sit and do nothing. No, I will work my very heart out to please my parents.

Although I must say, my first few weeks have not been easy. Many of the girls here are not like me. They think I speak in a strange accent. And I know I look different than them, with my long dark locks and my eyes like "pools of chocolate," as Nonna would say. On top of that, some of them have been living here at Eden College since they were four years old. I must seem very new and peculiar.

I need to go now for my classes. But I am anxious to write more, my new friend. My diary.

Elena

I read over the words again slowly. It was the diary of a girl! A girl who was 12, just like me! And also in her first year of school at Eden College.

She said some of her classmates had been there since they were four. I couldn't quite believe that Eden College used to take boarders from the age of four—so young! What else was there that I didn't know about my new school?

Suddenly, the door opened with a bang. Grace, Violet and Zoe came bundling in, hurriedly gathering their books for morning classes.

"What are you doing?" Zoe asked.

"I was reading the diary that I found in the bell tower with Grace. It's really old," I said.

Zoe looked over and nodded.

"Sounds really interesting, Ella, but I don't want to be late for class," Violet said, as she gathered her books.

"Maybe this diary will contain something secret— something I could write about for *Eden Press*!" I exclaimed.

"Come on, Ella, let's go," Grace said.

I wrinkled my nose. My friends didn't seem to share my excitement about my new find.

But I didn't care. I was going to read the diary of

Elena and see what mysteries she had to reveal to me. I was certain it was going to be something amazing.

Chapter 6

I was desperate to read more of Elena's diary, but at lunchtime I had an *Eden Press* meeting, so I couldn't do it then. I didn't want to carry the diary around with me either, as I was worried it was too delicate. So I had hidden it back under my pillow in my room.

As the bell sounded for lunch, I trotted through the main building to the classroom we usually met in for *Eden Press*. Now that I was the Junior Journalist (which meant I was in charge of all the news for Year 7), I didn't want to be late. As I scurried along the hall, I heard a voice call behind me.

"Ella! Wait up!"

I turned and saw Saskia jogging toward me. Saskia was also in *Eden Press*, and it just so happened that her sister, Ivy, was the Editor of the newspaper. At first I'd been a bit worried that Ivy would be like Saskia, but she wasn't at all. Ivy was a good leader. And a very good listener. She made coming to *Eden Press* really fun and she inspired us in our writing.

"So, what are we going to be focusing on for the next edition?" Saskia asked.

I had to admit, Saskia was being pretty good about me being the Junior Journalist. I wasn't sure if this was because she thought I'd be good at the job or because I didn't reveal a secret of hers in the last edition of the paper.

"Not sure. Let's go inside and see what the others think," I answered.

We entered the classroom, where Ivy and two other Year 9 girls were sitting at the head of the table with their laptops open. Ivy waved to us as we took a seat at the big square table. Slowly, the other girls who were part of *Eden Press* filed into the room.

"OK, it's great to see everyone!" Ivy said, clapping her hands to get our attention.

"I just want to say that everyone is loving the new look of the online paper. Our online data shows that our readership was up by 20% last edition. So, well done!" Ivy said. "And Ella, your piece was particularly well received. I think we need more of that stuff—human-interest pieces about what it's like to live here at school."

My cheeks flushed pink with pride.

"Everyone grab a marker and we'll start workshopping the next edition," Ivy said, tossing out marker pens.

Eden College had these cool tables, where you could write directly onto their surfaces, like a whiteboard. We could gather around and write our ideas on them, and then they would just wipe clean!

"I was thinking, what about a theme for this edition?" Ivy asked.

Everyone mumbled excitedly—a theme could be a

really fun idea!

Ivy smiled. "Suggestions?"

"Balance," a Year 8 girl said. "Like, show all the different areas of our life at Eden and do stories about how we balance everything."

Ivy nodded and wrote it down. Others started to shout out their thoughts.

"Recreation."

"Friendship."

"Mystery!"

"Ooh, I like that," Ivy smiled.

I thought about Elena's journal. I didn't want to tell everyone at *Eden Press* about it yet—not when I'd only just found it and didn't know what secrets it held. But I did have an inkling that there was going to be a great story in there.

"How about," I stammered, slightly self-consciously, "past and present?"

Ivy stopped and tilted her head to the side. Everyone else seemed to be thinking, too.

"I think that's a really interesting idea, Ella," she

said, as she jotted it down in the center of the table.

"I think it's a brilliant idea!" Saskia cheered.

Wait, what?

Ivy looked confused, clearly unsure if Saskia was being sarcastic.

Saskia laughed. "I really do! It fits in perfectly with the upcoming Alumni Luncheon!"

"What's 'alumni'?" one of the other Year 7 girls asked.

"It means a former pupil of a school or university," I said.

Ivy nodded. "Every few years we hold a special event at the school where students from the past come in for a reunion. We host a beautiful lunch and they speak about their lives. It's really interesting, actually."

"And the best bit," Saskia interrupted, "is that if you are a relative of one of the former students, you get to attend the special lunch with them. Everyone knows that our family have been Eden Girls for decades, so I think this is the perfect thing for me to report on!"

Ivy glanced over at me. I could see she was worried how I'd react, since the "past and present" thing was my idea. To be honest, it *was* a bit of a sting. I would have enjoyed reporting on the luncheon. But I still had Elena's diary, and who knew? Maybe that was going to be a way better story. I smiled and nodded.

"OK, I think that's a good plan," Ivy smiled.

We then broke up into our year groups to plan more of the other articles we might be able to do on this theme. Saskia's eyes were bright as she planned her piece on the Alumni Luncheon. She chattered about all the family members who would be coming along, including her great-grandmother.

I felt a pang of jealousy. Not because I wanted to show off people in my family who had been at Eden before me, but because I would have loved nothing more than to have a lunch with my mum and Nanna Kate and Great-Nanna Peggy all in the same room. I suddenly felt a lump in my throat, which I tried to swallow down. It was like an annoying piece of food lodged in my throat that also happened to make me want to cry.

These moments of homesickness and sadness weren't as common now that I was a bit more used to living at school. But every now and then, tiny things snuck up on me and made me think of my family, and while sometimes that made me happy, other times it made me really sad.

My Nanna Kate says sadness can be like that. She says sadness and happiness can get caught up in a tangle. The most beautiful of things can sometimes transform happiness to sadness in a moment—a whiff of your favorite flower, the first few notes of an old song or the feeling of grains of sand slipping through your fingers on a warm summer's day at the beach.

I swallowed hard and focused on our brainstorming session. Then the bell pierced through our chatter and we hurriedly gathered our things together for class.

"I hope I didn't upset you," Saskia said, as she put her pens back into her pencil case. She flicked her long, blond ponytail over her shoulder and stared at me with her piercing blue eyes.

"How so?" I asked.

"Oh, I mean with all my talk of how important my family is to Eden. I mean, my great-grandmother was one of the founding headmistresses, after all. And I get that it might make you a little jealous."

"I'm not jealous that your family has a history at the school," I laughed. "I just miss my family."

Saskia raised an eyebrow. "I guess you would say that," she said, shaking her head. "I mean, you probably don't understand just how special my family is here."

I decided not to argue with Saskia.

"Anyway!" she chirped, as she gathered up her belongings and skipped out the door.

I shook my head. Surely it didn't really matter that I had no history at the school. I mean, I didn't think Zoe, Grace or Violet did either—none of their mums or grandmas were Eden Girls. And nobody other than Saskia seemed to care about it. It wasn't really that important, was it?

Chapter 1

For once, I had no scheduled activities on after school. Zoe, Grace and Violet all had different things on, so it gave me the perfect opportunity to spend some time alone with Elena's diary.

I collected afternoon tea from the dining hall and then raced up to my room to retrieve the diary. I very carefully pulled the book out from under my pillow and carried it downstairs, tucked securely under my arm. I headed out the front door and onto Centenary Lawn, finding a quiet tree to sit under where nobody else was eating.

I bit into my apple, which was crisp and sweet. Then I placed it down beside me and wiped my hands on the sides of my dress. I gently opened the diary to the second entry and, as the warm afternoon breeze fluttered the pages, began to read.

4 February 1940

To my only friend, my diary,

Oh, how I long for a friend who isn't a book. Not to cause offense to you, my diary, for I love that you listen to my ramblings. But wouldn't it just be the loveliest thing in the world to have a true friend of my own?

The girls here are not so friendly to me. I know my accent is very different and sometimes they don't seem to understand me. Or perhaps they just pretend they can't.

I heard one of the girls, Hazel, whispering behind her hand and glaring in my direction. I wasn't sure exactly what she was saying, but the other girls who were listening looked at me with wide suspicious eyes.

I heard one phrase clearly, however: "can't be trusted."
Could that have been about me, dear diary? Why would
I not be trustworthy? Nonna says that trustworthiness
is one of the most important attributes of a kind soul.
And I always thought I was a kind soul.

It makes my heart heavy.

But, my diary, I have something of great excitement
to tell you among these ramblings of melancholy. I have
found something secret and special in the walls of this
very school! I was exploring through the quiet corners
of the main house, by myself, when I found it. I daren't
write where it is, lest someone read this diary and find
my secret place.

But, oh, what a wonderful discovery! A place of
solitude of my very own. A true secret find! And the
part I like the most is that it takes me out into the
surrounding environment. We are so carefully watched
here at Eden and I rarely get to go out into the trees
and skip among the birds, like I did back in my
homeland of Italy. So to find somewhere that gives me
secret access to nature—it is like a dream!

In other exciting news, Papa has written and said he is making me my very own special collection piece. His hands are like those of a creator of life—he crafts such beauty. I can't wait for him to send it.

I will leave you now, my diary, but will write again soon.

Elena

I frowned. There was so much in the entry that left me perplexed (that means very confused and curious). Why were the other girls whispering about Elena? Sure, she was from another country, but why would that make a difference?

The part that excited me the most was Elena's revelation of a "secret place," right here in the school! I wondered where on earth it could be! She mentioned the "main house." Was that the dormitory or the main building? And what was the "special piece" her father was making for her?

I felt like I had more questions than answers after reading Elena's diary entry. Everything in me wanted to race through the rest of her journal and see if I could find the answers, but I also wanted to take my time. I wanted to find as many clues as I could, hidden in Elena's words. And I wanted to savor the experience of reading the diary because it was just so interesting!

I pulled out my notebook and jotted down the most important things I'd discovered so far:

- *"Secret place" within the school—where is the "main house"?*
- *Why is Elena an outcast?*
- *Elena's Papa's "special piece"?*

"What are you doing?"

I looked up and shielded my eyes from the dipping sun to see the petite silhouette of Violet.

"Just reading that journal I found," I said to her.

She crouched down and reached her hand out. "Can I see?"

I felt my stomach flip. Of course I wanted to show her, but I was also very protective of the delicate old book.

Violet sensed my hesitation and laughed. "I'll be very careful."

I smiled and handed it to her.

"Wow, it's really old, isn't it? Anything interesting?" she asked.

"Not quite yet," I said cautiously. All I'd found so far were more questions. "But there could be."

Violet nodded and gently handed it back to me.

"How was Madrigals?" I asked. Madrigals was a superspecial singing group at Eden College. It wasn't just a choir, but a much smaller group for only the very best singers in the school. They had to sing lots of different parts without any background music. They often sang really old-fashioned songs, but they still sounded amazing. Violet was a beautiful singer with a stunning voice. I was constantly shocked that such big, majestic sounds could come out of such a tiny person.

"Good, thanks," she said. "I'm going to go inside and get a bit of homework done before dinner. Want to come?"

It was when she stood up that I noticed she was

carrying a large pearl envelope. It looked like it was made of special shiny paper—the kind you might get for a wedding invitation.

"What's that?" I asked.

"This? Oh, it's just my invitation to the Alumni Luncheon." She pulled the invitation out of the envelope and showed me. It was shiny, like the envelope, and had ornate, curly gold letters on it. It looked like an invitation to something with the Queen of England.

"But your mum wasn't an Eden Girl," I said, confused.

"No, she wasn't. And neither was my grandma. But my aunt on my dad's side *was* an Eden Girl. That's why my parents were so interested in this school. Apparently my aunt had the most wonderful experience here. So, she's coming to the Alumni Luncheon."

"Oh." I didn't quite know how I felt about that. "I guess you get to be one of Saskia's *special* group then," I said, rolling my eyes.

Violet tilted her head to the side.

"It's not a big deal, Ella," she said. "I knew about this weeks ago, when my aunt got her invitation. I didn't even think it was worth telling anyone about."

My cheeks reddened. "Well, as long as you don't go on about it, I guess. Anyway, to answer your question, yes, I'd love to come inside and get some homework done with you," I said quickly, trying to change the subject.

Violet extended her hand and helped me up. I dusted the stray leaves off the back of my dress and picked up my notebook and Elena's diary.

As Violet and I walked inside the dorm, I wondered why I had a bit of a tight feeling in my stomach. Surely I wasn't jealous that Violet was going to the luncheon, was I? Surely it wasn't that important.

But Saskia's words from earlier in the day echoed through my mind. Maybe I really wasn't special to Eden. Maybe this luncheon *was* important, after all.

Chapter 8

"Everyone, make sure you have your aprons on," Mrs. Finn said. "Hurry now, it's time to begin the lesson!"

We all fidgeted with our cooking aprons, tying them around our waists. The aprons were royal blue and had the Eden crest in teal on the front, to match our uniforms. I glanced over at Grace, who was standing at the counter with me and Zoe. Somehow, Grace already had a bit of flour on her face, even though we hadn't so much as touched any ingredients yet.

"I wonder what we are making today!" Zoe clapped, as she bounced up and down on her toes. Zoe and I love

Hospitality and Food Technology. It's a cool subject where we get to cook and bake and learn about the science of food. (That's the bit Zoe likes. I prefer the bit with cake.)

"I have some exciting news today!" Mrs. Finn gushed. Her round face was always beaming with happiness, and her thin silver-framed glasses bounced up and down on her tiny nose because she explained everything with such enthusiasm. My Nanna Kate always says you can tell what makes a person's heart sing. And for Mrs. Finn, it was definitely cooking.

"You all know that the Alumni Luncheon is coming up shortly. The exciting news is that Mrs. Sinclair has asked for our lovely Year 7 girls to act as waitresses and kitchen staff on the day!"

Saskia's hand shot up into the air. "But Mrs. Finn, what if we are *guests* at the luncheon?"

"Ah, yes, some of you will be attending the luncheon and will therefore not be expected to act as waitresses. You are free to spend time with your relatives who are guests with us on the day. But everyone else will be helping prepare and hand around the sandwiches, cakes and fruit to our guests."

"Oh, bummer!" Grace frowned. "I want to be a waitress!"

"But, you're not going to the Alumni Luncheon, are you? None of your relatives came to Eden—you said so yourself," I said, confused. I felt the blood rising to my cheeks.

"That's true, none of my family are Eden Girls. But my grandmother's sister—technically she's my great-aunt—was one of the vice headmistresses of the school. They always invite previous headmistresses and vice headmistresses along. So, Great-Aunt Clarice is coming," Grace said, wrinkling up her nose.

"Let me guess—you don't like her much?" Zoe laughed.

"Oh, she's always telling me I talk too much, and I'm too bouncy and fidgety, and I have terrible manners, and I'm always losing things, and I'm a disaster in the kitchen and I have no sense of *decorum,* whatever that means!"

Zoe giggled.

"It means having good manners and acting *properly*," I said quickly. "So, that means you get to sit at the tables and be part of the luncheon, while we all wait on you?"

Grace looked at me and her smile disappeared from her face. "It's not a big deal," she said flatly.

"Well, it sounds like *everyone* is going to be involved in this thing except me," I muttered.

"I'm not involved," Zoe said gently.

I shook my head. I knew I was being unfair to Grace. It wasn't her fault she had an invitation.

Mrs. Finn clapped her hands to get our attention. "There will be a catering company on the day, of course, but we will also be baking something for the luncheon. So, today we are going to have a practice run of making scones! Get into groups of three and stand together at one of the counters that already has the ingredients ready."

Zoe, Grace and I all looked at each other straightaway, knowing we wanted to be in a group of three. Even though it was a bit sad that Violet wasn't in our Food Tech class, it was probably a good thing, as it would have been awkward to make a group of three out of the four of us.

Mrs. Finn instructed us first to sit down with a pencil and go through the entire recipe, marking any necessary notes or questions in the margin. Zoe was meticulous about this. *Meticulous* means very thorough and detailed. And that's Zoe! She carefully highlighted each measurement to make sure we wouldn't make any mistakes.

"Come on, let's BAKE!" Grace jittered.

"Grace, you know what happened in Science when you weren't paying attention to the measurements," Zoe said in a serious voice.

Grace reddened. The bright-pink stain from Grace's last disaster remained on the science lab ceiling, even after the cleaners had spent hours trying to remove it.

Zoe measured out the flour and put it to the side while she measured out the milk. I cubed the butter with a knife, while Grace pulled out a bowl and a baking sheet and then preheated the oven.

While Zoe squinted over the recipe with her pen poised over the paper, Grace grabbed the flour and milk and dumped them in a bowl together.

"Grace, wait!" Zoe said, all too late. "We were meant to rub the butter into the flour first."

"Oh," said Grace. She shrugged, picked up the butter and dumped it into the bowl, too.

"Grace, no!" Zoe said, frustrated.

"Oh, it'll be FINE," Grace said, grabbing a wooden spoon and trying to mix the gluey concoction.

I winced. It didn't look right. "It's all lumpy," I said, peering into the bowl.

I looked at the counter in front of us, where Saskia, Portia and Mercedes worked their soft, smooth dough with a spatula.

Grace ducked down below the counter and started rummaging around in the cupboard. "I know what'll fix this," she murmured to herself.

"I think we should start again," Zoe said.

"No, no, this will fix it," Grace said cheerfully. She pulled out a blender and plugged it into the outlet on our counter. Then she picked up the bowl and began sploshing the mixture into the blender, causing soggy lumpy batter to spill down the sides. It was like clumpy glue.

"This should thin it out," she said.

Zoe and I looked at each other uncertainly. Before we could say anything, Grace's finger touched the dial of the blender.

"WAIT!" Zoe and I cried in unison . . . but it was too late.

The blender, which had no lid on it, erupted to life as Grace flicked the dial to full power. The sloppy batter shot up into the air, sending big, sticky white lumps raining down on us, as well as on Saskia, Portia and Mercedes. The three girls in front of us screamed in horror as their hair was coated with what can only be described as floury glue.

Saskia tried to pull a lump of dough out of her hair, but it stuck like a badly done papier-mâché craft project.

"Turn it off!" Mrs. Finn yelled over the top of the

whirring blender, which was still shooting batter up and out like a fountain.

I reached over and switched the power off at the outlet. Then I bleakly looked around at the disaster that was the Food Tech kitchen. Zoe, Grace and I were covered in batter and so were Portia, Saskia and Mercedes, who glared at us through narrowed eyes.

"Oops!" Grace said sheepishly. "Looks like I did it again!"

Chapter 9

When my Nanna Kate was younger, she decided one day to move to France. She said she had little more than the clothes on her back when she turned up there without a job. But she soon got work cleaning in a very famous opera theater.

Each night, she would wait in the wings while the performers sang the beautiful compositions. Afterward she would clean up the stalls, humming the songs she'd heard throughout the performance. But because she didn't speak French, she never quite knew what the opera was about. She could tell some parts were sad, some parts were passionate and some were triumphant. But she couldn't really appreciate it without knowing the language.

Nanna Kate said if you wanted to know about things in the days before the Internet, you had to go and find out with your feet. So she found a library, and in the library were audio tapes that taught you how to speak French. Each day, before the show, she would go and spend hours in the library, studying and learning and practicing the language. After many months, when the opera was coming to the end of its season, Nanna Kate decided she would listen again and see if she could understand.

She said once the language barrier had been broken, a whole new world opened up in that theater. Once she understood, she listened with tears streaming down her cheeks as she stood in the wings, waiting with her broom to sweep up the stage after the show.

And so, my Nanna Kate always says that libraries are "the fount of knowledge."

This is what I was thinking about as I walked up

the steps to the school library. I knew that if I wanted answers about Elena's diary, the library would be a good place to start my investigation.

I entered through the big glass doors and approached the front desk. Miss Mason was standing at the desk and greeted me with a warm smile. I knew Miss Mason because we had Library Studies with her once a week.

"Hello, Ella," she said. "Do you need any help finding a book? I have lots of good new ones to recommend."

I shook my head. "I don't need a fiction book today, Miss Mason. But I *am* interested in anything you have about Eden College's history."

Miss Mason frowned quizzically.

"For *Eden Press*," I clarified.

"Ah. Yes, come this way." She beckoned me with a wave and showed me around to a small corner of the library I'd never been to before.

"This is the archives," she said. "Here we keep all sorts of things about Eden's history, including old photographs, yearbooks, reports and maps. Is there anything specific you are looking for?"

I thought for a moment. I didn't want to tell Miss Mason about the "secret place" Elena mentioned in her diary, but I did want to know where I should look to find it.

"I'm wanting to see what Eden might have looked like in older times. I think it would be interesting for the Alumni Luncheon—you know, to do an article on how the school has changed since our oldest alumni left."

Miss Mason nodded. She pulled out some books, including one titled *An Eden History*.

"This one would be a good place to start—it has photographs and maps of the school before the newer parts were added," she said, opening up the book to show me. "Are you happy to have a browse?"

I nodded.

"Give me a wave if you need more help," she smiled.

As Miss Mason left, I pulled out my notebook and pen and flicked through the pages of *An Eden History*. Grainy tea-colored photographs of girls in thick long tunics and funny little hats peppered the pages. One photo showed a big old house, which I immediately recognized as our dormitory. It looked older and smaller—I was certain some additions had been built on since this photo was taken. But I could see the same entryway and the windows of the common room. Underneath were the words "Main house."

My heart skipped a beat. "Main house" was the exact term Elena had used about the location of her secret place.

I looked down at the words again. The paragraph described the downstairs of the building as the classrooms where the girls did their learning, whereas the upper levels were where they all slept. As I read on, it seemed that the girls slept on the first floor and the teaching staff slept on the floor above. So, there was a chance that Elena could have slept in the very same room I was now living in!

The thought gave me a tingle of excitement, as well as a feeling of unease—like a ghost from the past was looking over my shoulder. I shivered.

As I turned to the back of the book, I found old

photographs of the past year groups at Eden College.

I gasped excitedly—if I could find Elena's year group, I might actually *see* her face!

I hurriedly looked through the class pictures. I knew Elena was writing in 1940. And I knew she was in her first year of high school. By looking through the pages, I could see that the first year of high school was called Form 1 back then.

I glanced along the bottom of the grainy photographs, reading through the corresponding names. I didn't know Elena's surname, but I knew her first name at least. It didn't seem to be the most common of names.

But as I searched through Form 1 from 1940, I frowned. There was no listing of an Elena. I checked the photos for all of 1940, just in case her year group was called something else.

But there wasn't an Elena in sight. If Elena was writing from the dorm in 1940, she *must* have been a student in 1940. So why wasn't she in any of the photographs from that year? What happened to her?

I looked at my watch and realized how much time

had gone by while I'd been sitting in the library, flicking through the photos of past Eden. I packed up my belongings and began to walk back to the library doors—lunchtime was almost finished and the bell would sound soon.

"Did you find what you were looking for?" Miss Mason called out to me as I passed her desk.

"I did find some interesting things," I said. I thought through the other things on my list that I still needed to investigate.

"Miss Mason?" I asked. "Just off the top of your head, do you know if there was anything significant going on around 1940?"

Miss Mason cocked her head to the side. "Do you mean within the school or the world in general?"

"Well, either," I shrugged. I wanted to know what might have been going on in Elena's world.

"1940? Well, Ella, that was a very difficult time in history," Miss Mason said.

"Why?" I asked.

"1940 was during World War II."

Chapter 10

I sat on my bed and pulled out Elena's journal, hoping to find some more clues about her "secret place." I opened the worn pages delicately and flicked to where I'd last left off.

There had been several other entries that I'd read recently, but, disappointingly, they had shed no light on the mystery of the secret place. Elena had spoken more about feeling a little like an outcast and referred a lot to the "troubling times" they were in then. Now I knew she must have been referring to the war.

I smoothed open the tea-colored pages.

To my dear diary,

I almost revealed my secret place today—completely unintentionally, of course! I was walking along the landing of the first floor and had made it right to the far wall. I'd already shifted the panel and, just as I was about to crawl in, I heard someone coming up the stairs! I was able to shut the panel just as Cordelia reached the landing, but she eyed me suspiciously before going on her way.

I felt a pang, although I must say, people looking at me suspiciously is not something new. In these troubled times of war, everyone seems to have an eye for suspicion. I heard some of the girls at teatime saying that Papa was probably making equipment for the enemy in his workshop. So hurtful! Papa only makes things of great beauty.

Which brings me to my exciting piece of news! My gift from Papa finally arrived and it is more beautiful than anything I've ever seen him create! It is an Italian *sparrow brooch, and reminds me of the birds from home. It is made of pure, glistening gold and Papa has molded it so perfectly that the golden feathers look as if they should be soft to the touch. Of course, they are smooth and cold, as metal is, but from a distance they shimmer like the feathers of a real bird. The pin on the back is long and sharp, and fastens with what I can see is a clasp of high quality.*

I will wear it on my school dress with pride—a symbol of home.

I must go now, my diary.

Elena

I read back over the entry, my heart beating wildly. This was the most detail Elena had ever given in relation to her secret place. I knew from the library that the main house she spoke of was our dormitory. And in this entry, she spoke of a panel on the far wall of the first floor hallway. That was the very floor my room was on!

I leapt off my bed and peeked into the hallway.

There was no sign of Grace, Zoe or Violet, disappointingly. I wanted to share this secret and, hopefully, explore the secret place with my friends. But they must have all been at after-school activities. I was too anxious to start searching for the secret place to wait for them, so I went back into my dorm room and slipped my school shoes on.

I tiptoed down the hallway to the end of the corridor and looked at the wall blankly. There didn't seem to be a door or opening anywhere. I felt along the wall for some kind of secret catch or knob, but found nothing. I looked up, but the wall seemed to meet the ceiling in a very ordinary way—no cracks of sunlight peeping through. I frowned.

"What are you doing?" a voice asked from behind me.

I turned and saw Saskia and Mercedes walking toward their room, curious faces turned toward me.

"Oh, nothing," I stammered. "Just looking at the wall."

Saskia and Mercedes wrinkled their noses in confusion.

"It's part of my story for *Eden Press*," I said hurriedly.

"I'm looking at the architecture of the dorm."

"Sounds boring," Mercedes yawned.

Saskia's eyes narrowed and lingered on me a little longer, before she shook her head and followed her friend into her dorm room.

I breathed a sigh of relief.

Trying to look casual, I walked up to the other end of the corridor in the opposite direction to Saskia's room. Past the top of the staircase to the front of the building, I stopped and looked at the smooth wall there. I even ran my hands along it, looking for anything that might reveal a secret hiding spot. But there was nothing.

I breathed out, frustrated.

Then I looked back down the hallway to where I'd been before, and noticed the bathroom. I wondered.

Perhaps the bathroom was a new addition to the dorm, one that hadn't been there in older times. When you entered the bathroom, it extended beyond the wall at the end of the hallway. Perhaps the wall that was at the end of the hallway now was a new wall. Perhaps the hallway used to extend right to the end of the building, where the bathroom now stood.

I walked into the bathroom. A tap trickled water into the sink. There was nobody in any of the stalls or the showers. I walked across to the back of the room and examined the wall, which was paneled. I pushed each panel, hoping for some kind of clue.

As I reached the last panel, I noticed something odd. The bottom panel closest to the floor was not completely flush with the rest of the wall. I pushed it with both hands . . . and it moved slightly! I pushed harder, with my full weight on the wall.

The panel clunked, shifting back into the wall.

My eyes widened. I shoved the panel to the left and it slid along like a sliding door, revealing a gaping dark hole.

I coughed slightly as dust from the opening filled my nose. I pulled my phone out of my pocket and turned on the flashlight. Shining it inside, I saw something I wasn't expecting.

Old stairs.

I looked behind me, listening for anyone coming.

The coast seemed clear.

I had to duck right down low to get into the space, but, once I was through, I saw the headspace above me extended right to the upper levels of the house. I couldn't believe how much fit into what I'd always thought was just a thick wall.

I was nervous about going down the stairs. They were narrow and steep, and dropped down into the darkness below. Were they sturdy? What if I got stuck in here? Where did it lead?

But the journalist in me urged me on. I tested my weight on the top step, and, while it creaked a little, it seemed solid. I took the steps one by one, cascading down, down, down.

When I got to the bottom of the stairs, the space extended ahead of me in a tunnel. It smelled cold and earthy. I shone my phone up—I could see the wooden beams that supported the tunnel walls. I ducked down and felt the cold earth. It was pure dirt—there was no flooring on the ground at all.

I looked back up the towering stairwell—I was

certain that I'd traveled down past the lowest level of the house and was now underground. The thought was both frightening and exhilarating. Maybe I should go back? My chest felt tight with fear and excitement, all mixed together.

Then I felt a cold breeze whip through the tunnel. There must be another opening for a breeze to be coming through!

I walked cautiously through the dark tunnel, taking each step like a stalking cat, my eyes darting from side to side in alarm. All my senses seemed heightened. I jumped at the tiniest sounds.

I walked on and on, until, finally, I could see some light up ahead—natural light, not reflected light from my phone. I was relieved that it resembled sunlight. At the end of the tunnel was a small flight of wooden stairs built into the wall. It wasn't as high as the one I'd climbed down from the bathroom, though.

I tested the stairs with my weight and, although they groaned slightly, they seemed sturdy enough. I climbed them one by one. When I reached the top,

I saw an old wooden door with a latch above my head. Small pinpricks of sunlight broke through the tiny gaps in the wood. I pushed the latch with my fingers, but it wouldn't budge.

I really didn't want to have to walk back through the tunnel without finding out where it led, so I tried again. This time, the latch screeched and moved ever so slightly.

Buoyed with my small success, I tried again.

The latch clunked open with a metallic *CLANG*. I pushed up the door and sunlight flooded in, causing me to shield my eyes. I'd been down in the tunnel for some time and the light made me wince.

I climbed up through the hatch and found myself surrounded by trees. The door was flat on the ground and had largely been covered by dead leaves. I looked around. It was blissfully quiet and the smell of eucalyptus trees filled my nose.

I heard the cackle of a kookaburra nearby. It was like he thought it funny that somebody had finally found the secret passage of Eden College again.

I wondered who'd been the last person to walk that tunnel route?

I shielded my eyes from the sun and looked back in the direction I'd come. I could see the school wall in the distance, and the dormitory behind it. I realized the tunnel had led right out of the school grounds and into the bordering bushland.

My mind raced. I could be in a lot of trouble for being here without permission. Did anyone else know about the tunnel? Should I tell my friends? My teachers? Mrs. Sinclair, the Headmistress?

I took a moment to stand and breathe in the fresh afternoon air. The sun was slowly sinking down toward its chamber, but it was not yet gone for the day. The leaves of the gum trees were dry and crackly, and looked like they needed a good drink.

I imagined I was Elena—standing outside the school in the Australian bush. It must have felt so different than Italy. I thought about her traipsing through nature, alone yet somehow comforted by the company of the trees. Perhaps she felt less lonely outside among the trees than she did in the busy halls of Eden. I was sad for Elena.

It was getting late in the afternoon, so I decided I'd better get back to the dorm quickly. I didn't want to risk someone else finding the sliding panel, which I had left ajar. And I certainly didn't want somebody to shut it, locking me outside the school gate. Then I would be in a *lot* of trouble.

I hurried back into the tunnel, closing the latch behind me, and made my way back to school. I wasn't sure what I wanted to do with my newfound information, but I knew I definitely wanted to tell my friends first. This was big news!

Chapter 11

X —

From: <u>Ella</u>

Sent: Thursday, 5:48 PM

To: <u>Olivia</u>

Subject: HUGE DISCOVERY!

Hi Oliva,

Oh my gosh, oh my gosh, oh my gosh! Olivia, I've found
a secret passageway at school! It leads from the dorm
bathroom out into the bushland surrounding Eden!!
I HAVE to tell Grace, Violet and Zoe as soon as they get

back from their after-school activities.

What should I do with this info? If I tell the teachers, there's no WAY they will let us in there again. And who knows what else might be in the tunnel?

What would you do??

I gotta go—the girls will be back any second.

Love, Ella

I slapped my laptop shut and carried it out of the study room as I heard some girls walking in through the front door of the house. I recognized Zoe and Grace's voices, laughing up the corridor.

"Guys, quick, I have some news!" I gushed, grabbing their arms and pulling them up the stairs.

"Slow down!" Zoe protested, tripping on the stairs along the way.

Zoe and Grace followed me into our room and I shut the door behind us.

"Where's Violet?" I asked.

Grace shrugged.

"I have something to tell you guys," I said hurriedly.

"Hang on, hang on," Zoe said, pulling her sneakers off. "I only just finished cricket practice. I'm SO sweaty. Can't I take a shower first?"

"No, this is too important," I gushed, jumping onto my bed.

The door swung open and Violet walked in.

"Where have you been?" Zoe asked Violet.

"Drama Club. We've just started—"

"There's no time for that!" I yelled over the top of Violet.

"Settle down, Ella. That's pretty rude," Grace said, irritated.

I wrinkled my face. Why couldn't they appreciate that I had huge news to tell them?

"Go on, Violet," Zoe said.

"Well, we are doing a new production of—"

"No, you don't understand!" I protested. "I was doing some investigating for *Eden Press* and I found—"

"Ella, hang on just a minute," Grace said. "Why is *Eden Press* more important than Violet's Drama Club?"

"Because this is way more interesting," I smiled.

"Hey! That's mean," Violet said. "Why is *Eden Press* so much more interesting than Drama? For your information, I was about to tell the girls how I've been invited to do a soliloquy at the Alumni Luncheon in front of everyone," she said.

"A soli-what?" Grace asked.

"A soliloquy," I said. "It's like a solo speech from a play."

"That's awesome, Violet!" Zoe gushed. "I can't wait to see it!"

"But won't you be waitressing?" Violet asked.

Zoe and Grace exchanged knowing glances. The kind where there was a secret between them. A secret I clearly didn't know about.

"Well . . ." Zoe started. She looked at Grace, who shrugged.

"What is it?" I asked, momentarily forgetting about my epic news.

"I've been asked to host the Alumni Luncheon with the Year 12 School Captain," Zoe said. "You know, like welcome the guests and introduce the different segments. Using the microphone. They wanted someone in their first year and someone in their last year of school here to host it."

"OK," I said slowly. "So what's the secretive eyes about?"

Zoe looked at Grace, then looked down. "Oh, nothing. We just weren't sure how you'd react."

"What's that supposed to mean?" I frowned.

"Well, you seem pretty jealous that Violet and I are going to the luncheon with our relatives," Grace said.

"I am not!" I yelled. I felt the blood rising to my cheeks. I was NOT jealous.

"I just mean, you seemed weird about us getting invitations and we thought you'd feel left out if Zoe got one too, and you didn't," Grace finished.

"I don't even care about the silly luncheon," I said defensively. "Why would it even bother me?"

Violet, Grace and Zoe all looked at each other again. Another *knowing* look.

"Well," Violet said slowly, "you have seemed a little . . .

sensitive about Grace and Zoe's friendship lately."

"What? No, I'm not!" I yelled. "Like, how?!"

"Oh, it's nothing," Zoe said, trying to diffuse the situation.

"Well, it's clearly *something*," I shot back accusingly.

"Just little things," Grace said. "Like you seem annoyed whenever Zoe and I are partners for things."

"That is SO not true!" I shouted. A tremor in my voice betrayed my uncertainty.

Zoe put her hand out to touch my arm. I pulled it away sharply.

"What was your news?" she asked gently, clearly trying to change the subject.

"Nothing. It was nothing at all," I said, as I stood up angrily. I grabbed Elena's diary and my notebook and pen, which were neatly piled on the desk by the door. Then I stormed out of the room, slamming the door behind me.

Tears pricked my eyes. What kind of friends were they? Always leaving me out and talking about me. Not even wanting to hear my news. And then accusing me of being jealous? As if!

"Are you OK, Ella?" Ruby asked, as I stormed down the hallway.

"I'm fine!" I yelled back at her as I stomped past.

I ran all the way to the end of the hallway. Tears sprung from my eyes and dripped down my cheeks. I walked into the bathroom and slammed the door behind me. I looked into the mirror at my wet cheeks and puffy eyes.

I just wanted to go home. I wanted to be in my bedroom with my dog, Bob, listening to my favorite music, with Mum cooking dinner downstairs. I even wanted my annoying brother, Max, to come into my room to play a trick on me. Or Olivia to walk in demanding to borrow my gel pens. I wanted Dad to come in and tell me everything was going to be OK. But I couldn't have any of that because I was here at Eden College.

My chest heaved as I sobbed.

Then I heard footsteps and the familiar voices of Zoe, Grace and Violet echoing up the hallway.

"Ruby said she headed for the bathroom," one of

them said.

I looked around wildly. I didn't want to talk to them. I just wanted to be alone.

I pulled my phone out of my dress pocket and quickly turned the flashlight on. Then I ran to the secret panel and pushed it so it jolted inward. I slid the panel open and crawled in onto the top step. Then I slid the panel shut behind me.

Chapter 12

I bundled down the rickety stairs, almost tripping halfway down.

Calm down, I warned myself. The last thing I needed was to trip down the stairs in a secret passageway on my own. Imagine if I broke my leg and couldn't get help. I'd be stuck down here! Forever! Maybe I'd get eaten by wombats. I shuddered.

I walked along the dark, dusty passage, dragging my feet as I went. All I could think about was my so-called friends upstairs. They were probably talking about me again right now. About how I'm jealous and silly and just a big baby. Ugh!

I didn't even want to get to the other end of the tunnel. I just wanted to hide out in here forever.

As I dragged my feet along the ground, my toe clipped something in the dirt. It felt hard, like a pebble, yet thin, like a piece of metal. I shone my phone down into the dirt and dug about like a bandicoot in the backyard at night.

My fingers brushed something cold. It was definitely man-made. I picked it up and wiped the dirt off, exposing gold metal underneath. I used the hem of my uniform to polish it under the flashlight.

As I cleaned it, a beautiful, little metal bird revealed itself. It looked handmade, with tiny delicate strokes for feathers. On the back was a pin with a small clasp. It was a brooch.

A sparrow brooch!

I opened Elena's diary, which I was still carrying, and read back over the last entry. She had spoken about the gift her father had made her . . . a gold Italian sparrow brooch with a pin.

It must have been this brooch! My hands shook a little and I sat down heavily. It felt like I'd traveled back in time. I couldn't believe I was sitting here, in the very spot Elena must have sat, holding her precious brooch. She must have lost it down here.

I leaned up against the wall and decided to read the next entry in Elena's diary with the light on my phone. Maybe she would mention something else about the brooch.

8 March 1940

Oh, my diary,

   Things are getting worse. As news of the war spreads, life at Eden is getting harder for me. Everyone now regards me with much suspicion. I see them whispering behind their hands. And the words "untrustworthy" and "hidden motives" pepper their conversations.

   To make matters worse, I have lost my beloved Italian sparrow that Papa made for me. I wonder if it was stolen from me or if I was careless with the clasp. Either way, it is gone and I am inconsolable. There is only one other in existence—the one belonging to my dear sister.

My heart is heavy.

If only I had a true friend to share my sorrows with. But even the teachers regard me with watchful eyes.

Papa wrote to me and said things are equally fraught for him and my family in the city. Customers no longer come to his shop. I'm not sure I will be able to continue my education here if Papa is unable to sell his jewelry. What a tumultuous time we live in.

Elena

Poor Elena. I felt the heat of my anger at my friends start to ebb away. It was like watching glowing embers in the campfire as they slowly lose their heat and light.

But still, they *did* accuse me of being jealous. True friends didn't accuse each other of jealousy, did they?

Was I really jealous of Zoe and Grace's newfound friendship? I wasn't sure.

But at least I had friends, even if we were fighting. Poor Elena had no one. Only her diary . . .

That's why I really wanted to solve the mystery of who Elena was and why her diary ended up in the bell tower. I felt like I knew Elena—like she had become a part of me. I couldn't end things without knowing.

Plus, I wanted to know what secrets may have lived in the walls of Eden College. This could be an amazing thing to write about for my *Eden Press* article. But without any record of Elena in the school library, it seemed like she was some kind of ghost.

I shivered.

Uneasy now, I stood up and dusted the back of my dress to get rid of the dry dirt that was clinging to it from the floor of the tunnel. I gently tucked the sparrow brooch into my pocket.

Looking down at my phone, I noticed with alarm that the battery was running low. I suddenly felt a wave of panic wash over me—what if my phone ran out of battery and I was left down here in the dark? How would I find my way back?

I hurried back through the tunnel, toward the dorm. My phone beeped.

Battery less than 3%.

I breathed in sharply and carefully picked up my pace. I didn't want to run because it was so dark and the ground was so uneven. I finally made it back to the rickety staircase and began to climb. When I got to the top, I placed my hands on the panel and tried to slide it to the right.

It was stuck.

My heart started beating wildly—if this panel didn't open, I didn't think I had enough battery power to get back through the tunnel to the other end with my phone flashlight. I needed the panel to open *now*.

I banged on it, trying to loosen it a bit. Then I took a breath to calm myself, placed my palms flat against the panel and pushed.

"Come on," I whispered.

The panel moved half an inch.

I tried again. And again.

Finally, the panel shunted across its skirting and flung open with a bang. I looked into the bathroom, hoping nobody was in there. If someone saw me peeking out of the wall, they would have had the fright of their lives! And my secret would have been revealed.

Luckily, nobody seemed to be around. I climbed out and gently slid the panel back into place. Then I crept out of the bathroom, back toward my dorm room.

That night, I lay in bed looking up at the ceiling. I couldn't sleep. I hadn't spoken to Zoe, Violet or Grace all night. By the time I had gotten back to the dorm after escaping the tunnel, they had already gone to dinner, and at dinner I refused to sit with them or make eye contact. I could see them whispering and looking at me in a weird way. I bet they were talking about how jealous I was of them. Even though I wasn't. AT ALL.

It reminded me of the time that Olivia and I had a

massive fight. Mum had given me a superspecial top with a unicorn on the front for my birthday. The horn had glittery crystals all over it and Olivia immediately said she wanted one of her own. I was going to wear it to the school dance that weekend, but when the weekend arrived, the top had disappeared. Where on earth does a T-shirt go? I asked Mum if she'd put it in the wash and she said no.

I was sure Olivia had taken it. She'd already asked to try it on and I'd said no, multiple times. I yelled at her and told her I was never going to talk to her again if she didn't give it back. Olivia cried and said she didn't take it. So I stopped talking to her.

Later that day, Max and I were playing in the backyard when I saw something glistening in the bushes. I went over and there was my unicorn top, half buried in the dirt. Also in the hole were Max's missing dinosaur toys, Olivia's scrunchie and Bob's bone.

Turned out our dog had taken my top and buried it in the yard. Mum and Dad said I was too quick to accuse Olivia and I'd "really gotten the wrong end of the stick."

I didn't know what stick they were talking about at the time, but now I think they meant I'd made a big mistake.

When I went to say sorry to Olivia, I found her in her bedroom. She had a plain white T-shirt sitting on her desk, and she was carefully gluing sparkly crystals to it. She said even though she didn't take it, she wanted me to have something sparkly to wear to the dance.

I guess people can be wrong sometimes.

I thought about this as I lay in my dorm room, listening to the deep breathing and light snores of my friends.

Had I gotten this wrong, too? Were my friends right?

I drifted off to sleep and dreamt about secret tunnels with magical sparkly unicorns and muddy dinosaurs.

Chapter 13

✕ −

From: <u>Ella</u>

Sent: Friday, 8:10 AM

To: <u>Olivia</u>

Subject: Disaster

Hi Olivia,

It's a bit of a disaster here. Don't tell Mum—I don't want her to worry. But I've had a fight with my roommates. Yesterday, they accused me of being jealous of them. Jealous because they are all going to this silly lunch, called the Alumni Luncheon, and jealous because Grace and Zoe have been hanging out more. Can you believe it??!! It's like when you and Matilda had that fight last year.

I'm not really speaking to them. And I can see them whispering all the time, and glancing at me with secretive eyes. Probably talking about their precious luncheon. Or how I'm a jealous baby.

The problem is, when you LIVE at school you can't just go home and not worry about it.

What should I do?

I wish you were here.

Love, Ella

xx

I finished my email to Olivia, then went back up to my dorm room to get my things for school. I had Art for the first lesson of the day. This is usually an awesome thing—I love, love, LOVE art! But today it was not such an awesome thing, no, it was not. That's because Grace,

Zoe *and* Violet are all in my Art class, and I had been trying to avoid them. This is hard to do when you *live* with the people you are trying to ignore.

When the bell rang, we went to roll call, then headed straight off to the art studios. One of the great things about Eden College is the amazing facilities, and the art studios are no exception. They are big open rooms with huge square tables and stools sitting all around them. We have all sorts of equipment in there, too, like a kiln to bake our pottery and even a 3-D printer!

As I walked into the classroom, I saw that Grace, Zoe and Violet were already sitting in our usual place. Grace whispered something in Zoe's ear and Zoe looked at me. Violet waved to try and get me to come and sit with them, but I didn't want to. They were clearly whispering more secret things about me. Maybe this time it was about me being mean, as well as jealous. How was I to know?

I went and sat with my other friends, Ruby and Annabelle.

Mrs. Hodges blew into the classroom in a flurry, her

long skirts billowing around her ankles. Even though Mrs. Hodges' hair was completely gray, it looked more like shining silver. It was long and thick and just like I would imagine the mane of a unicorn. She always wore brightly patterned skirts and big interesting earrings. Today, her earrings looked like melting clocks, as if the clocks were going to drip right off her earlobes and land in a puddle on the workbench. She also always wore multiple bangles up each arm, which jingled and jangled whenever she moved.

"Good morning, girls," she said breathlessly.

"Good morning, Mrs. Hodges," we chorused.

"Today, we are doing something a bit different! We are going to take our sketchbooks out into the surrounding bushland so we can practice our nature drawings!" she exclaimed.

Everybody started to chatter with excitement. It was always fun to go outside during class time.

"Grab your hats and we will walk out the back gate of the school. There are some lovely quiet areas out there where we can sit and draw and *contemplate*."

We all put our hats on and trotted out the door in single file. We followed Mrs. Hodges out of the music, art and drama center and back down toward our dorm. Just ahead of me, I could see Zoe, Grace and Violet talking. I wanted to hear if they were talking about me, but I didn't want them to think I was listening. So I walked up to Saskia, Portia and Mercedes, who were walking just behind them.

"Oh, Ella," Saskia said in surprise. It wasn't often I approached her just to hang out.

"Hi, Saskia. Hi, Portia and Mercedes," I said cheerily.

"Hey," Portia and Mercedes said in confused unison.

"What are you up to?" Saskia asked, still surprised.

"I just wanted to hear about who you are bringing to the Alumni Luncheon again—it ties in with my *Eden Press* story," I said.

Saskia gushed. "Oh, *of course*," she said.

I knew this would keep Saskia talking—she loved telling everyone about her "Eden Family" and how important they all are. So, I could walk along beside her and listen in on Zoe, Grace and Violet's conversation easily.

"Zoe, your anklet is showing! You'd better pull your socks up before Monty sees it," I overheard Violet saying to Zoe.

"Thanks, Violet," Zoe replied. "It's actually a bracelet from my nonna, but it fits around my ankle. I had to wear it today because it's lucky. I always wear it to public speaking events, and I've got a debate at lunch. It stops me from getting stage fright."

"Well, keep it hidden," Grace warned. "You know how Monty feels about jewelry."

"So, are we all good for our plan later?" Zoe asked, lowering her voice a bit.

That was interesting. What plan? Sounded like something else I'd been left out of.

"Yep," Violet said. "I've got the supplies. Grace, have you—"

Grace turned and saw me standing directly behind them and quickly shushed the others. I raised my eyebrows accusingly. Grace went to say something, but I walked back to Annabelle and Ruby.

"Ella, wait!" Saskia called after me. "You haven't heard the end of my important story about my aunt!"

"Maybe later, Saskia," I said, annoyed. I was too upset to deal with Saskia right then.

Out past the back gate of the school, we wound our way through the bushland, along a thin, weathered track. The summer sun beat down on our hats and, despite only being early morning, I could feel a sticky sweat gathering on the back of my neck.

As we walked deeper into the scrub, all the human sounds started to ebb away and were replaced with the songs of the bush. A magpie warbled cheerfully and a kookaburra cackled. The dry eucalyptus leaves crunched beneath our feet and every now and then we'd hear a loud *SNAP* as somebody stood on a stick on the path. We eventually reached a clearing, which had a view out over a parched creek bed. It looked like water had not flown down the creek in many years.

"Stop here, everyone," Mrs. Hodges sang. "Now, find a quiet spot and start sketching! You can sketch the wider landscape or you can focus your drawing in on something small, like a gumnut or a bottlebrush."

I saw Zoe, Grace and Violet sit down near each other. My eyes met Zoe's and it looked like she tried to smile at me, but I turned away before we had time to interact.

As I looked around, I realized we were not too far from the secret tunnel exit, which was just on the other side of the creek bed. It couldn't be seen from where we were sitting, but I was certain it was there, as I had seen this part of the track when I'd come out through the tunnel just a couple of days ago. I squeezed my dress pocket, where the Italian sparrow brooch was sitting safely. It felt cold through the cotton material.

I pulled out my pencil box and opened my sketchbook. Just as I was about to start sketching the gum tree, a huge cockatoo flew down onto a branch right in front of me. It fanned out its bright yellow comb and looked directly at me, as if to say, "What are you doing here in my world?"

It stood so still, its dark-gray claws clutching the branch and its beady eye searing into me. So I quickly began to sketch it. I wanted to get its curious expression down in my sketchbook.

As I sketched away, I couldn't help but think of Elena. This was the area she liked to escape to—this was the place where she felt most at home. Without friends in the College, this was her refuge (that means her happy, safe place). Her friends were the birds and her music was the crunch of leaves underfoot and the hum of the cicadas in summer. This was her world. And here I was, some 80 years later, possibly sitting under the very same gum tree.

I glanced over to where Grace, Zoe and Violet were all sitting together. I felt a sting in my chest seeing them whispering together, as Grace threw her head back, laughing at her own joke. Is this how Elena felt every day? I wasn't sure. But I was certain of one thing: it wasn't a good feeling. Not at all.

Chapter 14

I awoke early on Saturday morning. We were allowed to sleep in on the weekend if we didn't have any sports matches. Breakfast was open until the later time of 9:00 a.m., which meant we could have a slower morning.

So I was surprised when I woke up to find our dorm room empty. I knew the Year 7 cricket team had a bye, which meant Grace and Zoe didn't have a match. Ordinarily, if they had nothing on they would sleep in, especially Grace. My watch blinked 7:45 a.m. and yet our room was deserted.

Maybe my friends just wanted to get away from me.

I decided to have my shower before breakfast today, to beat the rush later. That's one downside to living with a whole bunch of girls—there's always a line for the showers.

I padded up the hallway in my pajamas and slippers, carrying my towel and my toiletry bag, which contained my shampoo, conditioner and body wash. I was enjoying the unusual silence around me. Everyone must be still asleep or already at breakfast.

As I entered the bathroom, which was completely empty, I couldn't help looking across to the panel behind which the secret passage was hidden. It was like a quiet ghost calling me. I walked over to the panel and gently placed my hand on it. It was cold. When I put my ear to the wall, I could hear the faint whoosh of the wind sweeping through the tunnel.

Smiling, I hopped into a shower cubicle, turned on the warm water and let it wash over my head and face. It was nice not having a line of people yelling at me to hurry up, like on weekdays.

A million thoughts rushed through my head. I thought about my friends and where they could be. I thought about how I missed them, even though I was still mad at them.

Then I thought about Elena. I felt sad for her, that she didn't even have friends to miss. And why wasn't she in any of the Eden College records for 1940? Her journal clearly said 1940. Where had she disappeared to?

When I finished my shower, I grabbed my towel from the hook on the door and dried myself all over, before wrapping it around me. I slipped my feet into my slippers, gathered up my belongings and headed back up the hallway to my dorm room. I opened the door, expecting to see at least one of my roommates, but the room was still quiet and empty. I frowned.

I pulled out a pair of shorts and a T-shirt from my chest of drawers. Being a weekend, we could wear whatever we wanted, and I could see it was going to be another hot summer's day. Maybe I would go for a swim in the school pool later today. I bundled my damp hair into a messy bun on the top of my head and slipped on my flip-flops. As I walked back into the hallway, it was still eerily quiet.

I went downstairs, out the main doors and across to the dining hall. Inside, there were plenty of girls chatting and eating, but it didn't have the same busyness as a weekday. Some girls had taken their toast outside to eat in the morning sunshine, others sat at the long benches in the dining hall eating cereal, fruit or pastries (which were a weekend treat).

I grabbed a bowl and heaped some muesli and fruit into it, along with a splash of milk and a dollop of thick, creamy yogurt. Then I turned and saw Grace, Zoe and Violet sitting together at the end of one of the tables. I hesitated. Should I go over?

As I approached, I saw Zoe look up. She hurriedly nudged Grace and signaled to Violet to stop talking. All at once, they stood up and took their empty bowls and plates to the kitchen area, before bustling out the dining hall doors. My heart lurched in my chest. Was this how it was going to be from now on?

I sat by myself near a group of Year 8 girls, who chattered away happily, not even acknowledging my existence. My muesli felt heavy and unappetizing. I scooped up a final mouthful, deciding I didn't want the rest. I slowly took my bowl up to the kitchen area.

"Not hungry today?" one of the servers asked, as she scooped my leftover breakfast into the compost bucket.

I shook my head.

What was I going to do now? I had a whole weekend ahead of me and no friends to spend it with. I walked back into the dormitory and up the stairs. Grace, Zoe and Violet had probably already left to go do something together for the day. I turned the doorknob to my room and slowly pushed it open.

"SURPRISE!"

I squealed with fright and jumped backward into the hallway.

Inside, the room was decorated with streamers and balloons. Hanging over my bed was a homemade sign, written in glitter pens, saying:

We ♥ Ella!

"Wha—what's this?" I stammered. "It's not my birthday . . ."

"We know," Zoe said, running over to hug me. "We just wanted you to know how much we love you and that we are sorry for calling you jealous."

I looked up and Grace and Violet were nodding in agreement.

Beside Grace, on the desk in our room, was a plate of chocolate chip cookies.

"Where did these come from?" I laughed.

"From my Food Tech class," Violet said. "We were making them as practice for the Alumni Luncheon. We got to take them with us though. So it's officially a party," she laughed.

She offered us each a cookie and we all took one. Violet herself probably wasn't able to have that much sugar in one go. I bit into the cookie, which had just the right amount of crunch while still being soft in the center.

"So, is this what you were secretly whispering about in Art class?" I asked, suddenly feeling guilty.

"Yes," Violet said. "We wanted it to be a surprise, but then we realized it was probably making you feel even worse! Sorry for that, too."

"You guys are the best," I said, my eyes becoming teary. I hugged each one of them and said I was sorry for storming off.

I really did have the best friends anybody could ask for. I felt guilty about comparing their behavior to what Elena experienced in her journal. My experience of Eden College was nothing like hers.

Thinking of Elena made me suddenly realize that I'd never shared my big news about the secret tunnel with my friends. I blurted out everything I'd discovered over the last few days—from the mystery of Elena not appearing in any Eden records to her journal entries about a secret place. Zoe, Violet and Grace listened with wide eyes. The idea of a hidden passage somewhere in the school was as shocking and exciting to them as it was to me when I first read about it.

"So, did you find it?" Grace blurted.

I looked at them all with a very serious face.

Then I nodded.

All three of them squealed at the same time, bombarding me with questions about where it was and what it was like.

"I could tell you," I said slowly. "But wouldn't you prefer for me to *show* you?"

"Ella, are you playing a trick on us?" Zoe moaned, as she stood by the bathroom door.

"Just keep watch!" I hissed.

Grace and Violet stood next to me by the panel as I tried to slide it open. It was still stiff from the last time I'd come through, when I'd almost been stuck inside.

"It's just a little stiff," I puffed, as I leaned on the panel with all my weight. I knew the door had to push inward first before it would slide along its runner.

"Are you sure this is the right spot?" Violet asked. I could see the doubt in her eyes.

"It is!" I protested, as I tried to ram the panel with

my shoulder. "It was working the last time I came."

"Mayday! Mayday!" Zoe called from the entryway to the bathroom. Someone was coming!

A tall figure pushed open the door and strode into the bathroom. It was Ms. Montgomery.

"What is all that banging?" she demanded.

Zoe, Grace, Violet and I looked at each other, mouths agape, unsure what to say.

"The door was jammed—" I began at *exactly* the same time as Grace said, "The window was jammed—"

I winced.

Ms. Montgomery frowned. "Well, which was it? The door or the window?" She narrowed her eyes in suspicion.

"I meant the door, the door of the stall," Grace bumbled.

Ms. Montgomery reached for the stall door that was closest to us and swung it easily on its hinges. "It seems fine to me," she said, raising one eyebrow.

"Oh, it is *now*," Zoe said. "But before, it was stuck and Violet was in there."

Violet nodded furiously.

Ms. Montgomery looked at each one of us through narrowed eyes.

"Well, you are clearly fine now, so be on your way," she said. "And in the future, call an adult for help if you are stuck—don't go crashing and bashing school property."

"Yes, Ms. Montgomery," we chorused, as we filed out of the bathroom.

She watched as we walked back down the hall.

"So much for that idea," Zoe said, irritated.

"I think we are going to have to wait awhile before we try that again," Violet said. "She's on to us."

We all nodded, disappointed. All I wanted to do was share my secret with my friends. But for now, it would just have to wait.

Chapter 15

12 March 1940

My dearest diary,

Well, the worst has come to pass. The fateful day has arrived. Papa is coming to pick me up. There has been nothing organized to bid me farewell. All I know is that I am leaving Eden, not with fanfare but with a whimper.

I think this is a reflection of our world at this time—relationships quietly stuttering to a standstill, like the snuff of a candle. As the bombs shine brightly, the flame of friendship grows dim. Such troubled times.

I write this entry from one of my favorite places in the school—up high, where I can look down, like a bird in the sky, and see everything. I come up here a lot to think and reflect.

Despite my somewhat sad time within these grounds, there is also something I love about this place. I am sad to leave, I will be honest. Perhaps, in another life, another time, things would have been different here.

Oh! I hear the quiet *putt, putt, putt* of Papa's vehicle. I can see it coming over the hill and winding up the dirt road that leads to the school. This is it. My final moments at Eden College.

But I vow to return.

So, I am going to hide you in this special place, my dear diary, knowing that I will come back for you one day. I have found in the past a secret little place for you, behind a loose brick up here in the bell tower.

I can hear the Headmistress calling my name. I need to hurry.

Sleep peacefully, my dear diary, until I return.
One day.
One day.
Elena

What?

That can't be it?! I flicked ahead in the journal to see only blank pages.

How can this be the end of Elena's diary?

I ran my hands through my hair in frustration. I had no answers! Why did Elena leave? Where did she go? Why is there no record of her at the school?

Clearly her last entry was all about hiding her journal in the bell tower. The fact that it was still there for me to find told me Elena probably did not make it back to Eden College. But why not? It all felt so . . . so unresolved (that means it wasn't tied up neatly at the end like a good *Millie Mysteries* book).

I sighed in anger.

Elena's story had become so dear to me. How could I possibly end it without ever knowing what happened?

And I wanted to write about this for *Eden Press*. But now I had no story. There was nothing here to write about—nothing about Eden College in the 1940s. No ending for a lost girl named Elena. She had just vanished, like thistledown on a summer's breeze.

And to make matters worse, we hadn't been able to get back into the secret tunnel. Being a Sunday, there were girls all over the dorm. We couldn't get a minute alone in the bathroom without someone barging in.

And when we finally did get a few seconds, we found that the panel was still jammed in place. Grace had suggested accessing the tunnel from the surrounding bushland, but there was no way we would be able to go outside the school gate without one of the teachers seeing us. I felt completely locked out—just like I did reading the end of Elena's journal. Everything felt like one big dead end.

"Why so down?" Grace asked, walking into our dorm room.

I looked up, still seated on my bed. "Elena's journal just ends! She hides it in the bell tower, but there are no answers. I don't know why she left, where she went or if she ever came back."

"Maybe there are no answers. Maybe she left the school and that's all there is to tell," Grace shrugged.

"But I feel like there's more," I said, shaking my head. "I mean, there *has* to be more to this story than that." I winced, frustrated. "Nobody just disappears."

"I know what will cheer you up. How about a trip into town?" Grace said. "Maybe a milkshake?"

"We need a Year 9 to go with us," I reminded her.

"Well, let's go find one then!" she said, extending her hand out to help me up off the bed.

I groaned. But Grace was right. I needed something to take my mind off Elena's unfinished diary.

We walked along the corridor, looking for a Year 9 student. One was coming up the stairs.

"Andrea, want to accompany us into town?" Grace asked.

"Not now, Grace," she said. "I'm going to play tennis."

We kept walking along the hallway, checking the

rooms for Year 9 students along the way. We peered into Saskia's room and there on her bed was her sister, Ivy. The two were playing cards together.

"Ivy!" Grace chirped. "I don't suppose you feel like accompanying some *adorable* Year 7 girls into town? Maybe get a milkshake?"

"Ooh, sounds fun!" Saskia beamed.

My heart sank. Of course we had to invite Saskia. It would be rude to steal her sister away and not invite her. But I just wasn't in the mood for her drama.

"Sure," Ivy said. "Let's go, Saskia!"

"Do you mind if we see if Violet and Zoe want to come, too?" I asked.

"The more the merrier!" Ivy smiled.

We all went down to the common room and found Violet and Zoe watching TV. They were more than happy to escape to town and ran back up to the dorm room to get their wallets.

Ivy checked with Monty that it was OK to go and we all signed ourselves out in the attendance log.

When Grace said we were going into "town," what

she really meant was a tiny collection of local shops, about a five-minute walk from school. There was a small supermarket, a post office, a hairdresser and a fish-and-chips shop. The fish-and-chips shop doubled as a café and ice cream parlor, and we'd often get ice cream or milkshakes there on hot weekends.

"Hi, Arnold!" Ivy said to the shop owner as we walked inside.

"What will it be today, girls?" Arnold replied.

Arnold was a large, rotund man who had owned the shop for years. His father had worked there, too, and his father before that, so it had been a family-run business for many generations.

We all ordered milkshakes and sat out in front of the shop on the shiny, metal outdoor furniture.

"So, are we all ready for the Alumni Luncheon tomorrow?" Saskia asked, as we sipped our milkshakes.

I rolled my eyes. I'd heard enough about the luncheon.

"I can't *wait* for my mum and grandma to come," she gushed.

"Ugh, that means my great-aunt will be here in the morning," Grace said, scrunching up her nose.

"It also means I need to be ready to host the event," Zoe said in a wavering voice. "I'm so nervous."

"You'll be great, Zoe," Violet said. "I'm pretty nervous about the drama soliloquy I'm doing, too."

"Sounds like we all have pretty important things to do," Saskia said. "Oh, sorry, not meaning that you are *not* important, Ella," she said in fake sympathy. "Waitressing is important, too, I guess."

I rolled my eyes.

"And you never know," Ivy interrupted. "You may get some good material for your *Eden Press* story," she smiled. Ivy was so kind. Sometimes I couldn't believe she was Saskia's sister, even though they had the same cascading blond ponytails and shining blue eyes.

"I don't have much of a story yet," I said in all honesty. "I'm running out of time."

"Don't worry," Ivy said. "Sometimes the right story just takes a bit of time to brew."

I hoped Ivy was right because right now I had

nothing. I wasn't doing anything at the Alumni Luncheon and the big mystery of Elena's journal had hit a dead end.

I needed something and I needed it fast.

Chapter 16

There was a buzz of excitement in the air on Monday morning. We had all been told to make sure every room in the school was clean and tidy. We'd even made sure there was no rubbish lying around the school grounds, and the groundskeepers had worked extra hard to manicure the hedges and the lawns. It was a beautiful, bright sunny day, which made things all the more pleasant for the day ahead.

The Alumni Luncheon guests had started to arrive around mid-morning and were enjoying tours of the school, guided by the Year 11 and 12 students. Since all the guests had either attended or taught at Eden, it gave them great joy to see how the school had transformed and evolved over the years.

We had been sent back to the dorm after our morning lessons to neaten ourselves up before the luncheon. Grace was spending an unusual amount of time in front of the mirror, making sure her French braids were perfect. She tied them off with shiny, satin white ribbons and inspected herself in front of the mirror. She smoothed her hands over her uniform, straightening the collar and pulling up her knee socks.

"Do you think my socks look off-white? They are meant to be white. Not just white. Crisp white. White–white. Are they white?" she said at great speed.

Violet and I giggled. Grace always spoke quickly when she was nervous.

"Yes, they are *white*," Violet laughed. "Is this all because your great-aunt is going to be here?"

Grace wrinkled her nose. "You have no idea what she's like!"

Zoe paced around the dorm room, reading from

her notes. "It is my honor and pleasure to welcome you here today, to the Aluminum Luncheon. No, not aluminum," she stumbled, "I mean *Alumni* Luncheon. Ugh!"

"Zoe, calm down," I said, giving her a pat on the arm. "You'll be *fine*. Just breathe."

Zoe nodded and frowned, and then began pacing again.

"Well, at least you are all doing something important," I said, as I tied my apron around my waist. "I'll be stuck in the kitchen putting jam on scones."

"I'd rather be there than with my Great-Aunt Clarice," Grace said.

"She can't be that bad," Violet laughed.

"Oh, you just wait," Grace said with wide eyes.

We put the finishing touches to our hair and uniforms, then walked downstairs and out the front door. The Alumni Luncheon was taking place in the function hall, up in the main part of the school. It was a big room that the College used for events, with a kitchen attached for catering.

As we neared the function hall, we saw that some of the alumni guests were already wandering around the central courtyard, admiring the water fountain.

"Look how it's changed!" an older lady gushed to the women standing around her. "Yet I see the bell tower is still there, just the same as in my day!"

We leaned casually on the fountain wall, but I noticed Grace's eyes darting wildly around the courtyard. She bounced nervously—even more than usual.

"Grace, you look stressed," I said.

"I'm just keeping an eye out for my great-aunt. She sneaks up on you, like a ninja," Grace whispered.

"I'm sure she's not that bad—"

"Grace Alessandra!" a stern voice bellowed from behind us.

We all jumped to attention.

"Oh, how you slouch, my girl!" the voice said.

We turned to see an older lady in a long navy skirt. She wore a white blouse, buttoned right up to her chin, and the long sleeves were also buttoned at the cuff, despite the hot day. There were ruffles down the front of her blouse and a necklace of pearls around her neck. She leaned on a cane, which was black with a rubber stopper on the end. Her skin was crinkled, like a used tissue, but her gaze was severe. Her green eyes were beady and accusing. It could only be one person . . .

"Great-Aunt Clarice!" Grace exclaimed in clearly insincere excitement. "How lovely to see you again!"

"Stand up straight!" she barked.

Grace stood tall, her hands clasped behind her back.

"Well, aren't you going to introduce me to your friends?" Great-Aunt Clarice asked.

"Of course," Grace stammered. "This is Ella."

"How do you do?" I said.

"And Zoe."

"Pleasure to meet you," Zoe said.

"And this is Violet."

"Nice to meet you," Violet said in a meek voice.

"This one is too small for high school," Great-Aunt Clarice said, nodding at Violet.

Violet shrunk back at the shock of her rudeness.

"And you two, pull your socks up," she barked at me and Zoe.

We looked down at our socks, which were already neatly pulled up our legs and folded correctly at the cuff.

"But—" Zoe began.

"Of course, they will," Grace said hurriedly, urging us to correct our already-perfect socks.

"When I was Vice Headmistress of this school, the standards were *much* higher," she scoffed. "None of this untidiness and slovenly behavior."

Grace frowned in confusion at the word *slovenly*. I almost explained it means untidy and dirty, but I figured it probably wasn't the time.

"Great-Aunt Clarice, can I show you inside?" Grace asked.

Great-Aunt Clarice turned up her nose and followed Grace into the function hall. Poor Grace looked like she was walking with a pile of books on top of her head.

We followed Grace into the function hall, where some of the other guests for the luncheon were already milling around. The hall had been beautifully decorated, with the chairs in crisp, white fabric covers that matched the table clothes. There were ornate flower arrangements on the tables and the smell of jasmine wafted through the air.

Grace stood still as her great-aunt picked at her hair and tried to straighten out her dress. Even from a distance, I could feel Grace's discomfort. Poor Grace.

"Ella, I'm going to go get ready for my soliloquy," Violet said, as she dashed back out the door.

"How are you feeling about hosting the luncheon?" I asked Zoe. Zoe didn't look her usual shade of olive brown, instead her skin looked a pale yellow. I knew this meant she was super nervous.

"OK," she said slowly. "I should probably go up to the front to Mrs. Sinclair and Lauren, the School Captain, to check that everything is in order. Lauren and I will be welcoming everyone to the luncheon soon and I have to give a short speech about what it has been like for me joining Eden this year."

"You'll be great," I said, pulling her in for a quick

hug. "And I, in the meantime, need to go to the kitchen like a poor little Cinderella who has not been invited to the ball!"

Zoe laughed. "But remember how that story ended? Cinderella turned out to be the most royal of all." Zoe squeezed my hand and let me go.

I walked into the kitchen, where the air was buzzing with activity. The kitchen staff were hurriedly preparing finger food for the lunch, and the Year 7 girls who were not directly involved in the luncheon were helping them out.

The catering manager looked at me and said, "Go check your name off on the list and it will tell you which group you are in."

I nodded and went to the bulletin board at the entrance of the kitchen and ran my finger down the list of names. There were lots of jobs listed beside each name, ranging from sandwich making to scone preparation, escorting guests to their seats to handing out the food. I spied my name and then groaned as I saw the group I was in.

Dishwashing.

Ugh! Now I really did feel like Cinderella! I couldn't believe I was going to be spending the day washing plates and teacups. I looked over toward the sink and saw it was already full of metal bowls and wooden spoons, which had obviously been used for making the scones and biscuits earlier that morning.

What a laborious task! *Laborious* means tiresome and unexciting, and that's exactly how I felt about the day's duties ahead of me.

I sighed.

Suddenly, the door burst open.

"No running in the kitchen!" the catering manager yelled gruffly.

I looked up and saw Zoe. Why was she in the kitchen? She looked around, uncharacteristically frazzled. I could see tears streaking down her cheeks and her nose looked pink and a bit runny. I rushed up to her.

"Zoe! What's happened? Why are you so upset?"

"Oh, Ella, it's terrible," she sniffled, pulling a tissue

out of her dress pocket. She blew her nose and dabbed her eyes. "I can't do this. I can't host the luncheon!"

I looked at my friend's face. Her green eyes shimmered with tears as she looked pleadingly back at me. "Zoe, you will be fine," I reassured her. "You've spoken in front of a crowd many, many times! You are one of the best debaters in Year 7—this is no worse than standing up for a debate."

"It's not that," she said, fresh tears welling up in her eyes. "It's my anklet. The good-luck anklet my nonna gave me. I've lost it! And I've never done any public speaking without it!"

"Well," I said slowly, "are you sure you've had it at every single debate? You must have done some debates without it, and that went OK, right?"

"Wrong!" she cried. "I forgot it once and completely messed up. I can't do it without it."

I knew this wasn't the truth. Zoe *could* do the speech without her anklet. But I also knew that I had no time to convince her of that. As my Nanna Kate says, sometimes, when somebody has a truth so firmly implanted in their head, you just have to run with it.

"Where did you have it last?" I asked.

"I don't know," she said, shaking her head.

I thought. "You had it when we went into the bush for Art class," I said. "Remember? Grace told you to tuck it into your sock. Did you have it later that day?"

Zoe frowned as she retraced her steps through that day. "I don't think I did," she said. "I must have lost it in the bush! I remember pulling my socks down while we were drawing so I could get some sun on my legs."

I swallowed hard and looked at my watch. There was no time to get permission to go searching through the bush. Monty would never allow it. And there was no way to sneak out there to look . . . or was there?

"I'm going to find it for you," I said, pulling my apron off over my head.

"What, how?" Zoe stammered.

"I'll use the secret passage. Don't worry, Zo, I won't let you down."

"But, Ella, there's no time—" Zoe began to shout after me.

I didn't hear what else she had to say. I was already on my way out the door. I had to help my best friend.

Chapter 17

I tore through the grounds of the school, back toward the dormitory. I knew I could get into trouble for this, but my best friend really needed me. I ran across the lawn in front of the dorm, leaping over the flower beds and taking a shortcut across the rose garden, which is out of bounds. Then I ran through the front door of the house.

It was eerily quiet. I knew most of the students were already at the Alumni Luncheon, either entertaining their guests or helping out. And the rest of the school would have been in class. Technically, I wasn't allowed to be in the dorm at this time of the day.

I ran up the steps, taking them two at a time, and sprinted up the hallway toward the bathroom. I burst through the doors, looked around and was relieved that nobody else seemed to be in there. I stopped to catch my breath, and only then did I notice that the final stall door was closed. The toilet flushed and someone turned the lock.

"Ella, what are you doing here?" Saskia asked as she stepped out.

No!

"I just wanted to neaten myself up before the luncheon," I mumbled. I knew it was a lame excuse, and, judging by Saskia's face, she thought so, too.

"I was just collecting some of my work to show my family, who are here today. It's such a *special* day for us," she gushed.

"Sure is," I said quickly, willing Saskia to leave.

She washed her hands slowly.

"I saw on the list you are in the dishwashing crew!" she cackled. "It's so unfair for you."

I breathed in deeply, biting my tongue.

"I mean, it's just not fair you are stuck in the kitchen with the grime and the soapsuds, while I get to be at the luncheon like a princess!" she said.

"Yep, it's a Cinderella story, that's for sure," I said. "Are you done here?"

Saskia frowned. "Well, yes, I am, thank you, bossy boots." She dried her hands and clopped huffily out of the bathroom, letting the door swing shut behind her.

I let out a breath of relief. That was close. Thankfully, I knew Saskia would be too busy being "queen for a day" to think about what I might be doing in the bathroom.

I walked over to the panel and tried to slide it along the runner. It didn't budge. I remembered last time: it had to be pushed in a bit first before it would slide. I pushed hard, but the panel remained in place. I pounded it with my fists, but again, it didn't budge. I tried using all my weight, pushing with my shoulder, to make it move, but no matter how hard I tried, it was still stuck firm.

I frowned. I thought of Zoe, tearily relying on me back at the function hall. I thought of Saskia, parading around like she owned the school, making everyone feel inferior. And I thought of young Elena, without a friend in the world, yet being brave nonetheless. I channeled my anger about it all, summoned my energy and karate-kicked the panel.

It indented slightly.

Yes!

Now that it was pushed in, I hoped it would slide smoothly along the runner. It made a scraping noise as I shunted it along, but it was definitely moving.

Once the opening was large enough for me to climb through, I slipped into the hole, onto the top step of the hidden staircase. I turned my phone flashlight on and carefully walked down the rickety treads. When I reached the firm ground of the tunnel floor, I picked my pace up into a jog.

As I came to the end of the passageway, I could see a sliver of light coming from between the slats. I crept up the stairs and gently pushed on the door latch.

Just as I was about to fling it open, I heard the crunching of leaves. It was the sound of footsteps.

I froze. Who would be out here in the bushland surrounding Eden College?

I peered up through the cracks in the door to try to see who it was. But being below ground level, I could only see a few inches above me.

I heard the footsteps getting louder. They sounded like someone walking slowly. Perhaps limping.

Then I heard a voice.

"I don't think it's here," a man said.

"It is!" a crackly voice replied. It sounded like an old woman.

"You shouldn't be out here. Come on, let's go back. It's almost time to start," the male voice said.

"I'm not crazy, you know," the older voice snapped.

I kept the door almost completely closed, holding my breath as the two people walked away from where I was hiding.

Who could that have been? And what were they looking for?

When I was certain the people had gone, I flung open the door and climbed out of the passageway. The sunlight burned my eyes after being in the dark for the previous few minutes.

I began looking around the area we had been drawing in Art class a few days before. I tried to remember where Zoe had been sitting. But the bush all looked the same.

Suddenly, a huge cockatoo flew down, squawking at me and giving me a fright. It landed on a branch and looked at me curiously. It nodded, as if encouraging me. Then I remembered—this was the exact place where I had been sketching the cockatoo for my drawing! And if I had been sitting here, then Zoe would have been over to the left with Grace and Violet!

I rushed across the clearing to where I remembered my friends sketching together the other day. I kicked the dirt and leaves from side to side, furiously trying to find any glimpse of Zoe's anklet. I stepped up to the log they had been sitting on and rolled it to one side slightly. Grubs and bugs squirmed around in the moist undergrowth, but there was no sign of the anklet. I walked toward the bush path, which we had taken to get back to school. I kept looking and looking. But it was no use.

Just as I was about to give up, the cockatoo let out another ear-piercing squawk. I turned to see it standing on a branch just behind me. It was nodding vigorously.

I'd never seen a cockatoo act this way before. My eyes dropped to the foot of the tree he was perched on, and I caught a flash of light. I ran over to the base of the tree and rummaged through the leaf litter with my fingers.

My fingers caught on something in the dirt. It was cool and metallic—a chain! I pulled it up out of the ground and dusted it off. It was Zoe's anklet!

I couldn't believe I'd found it!

I looked down at my watch and realized the luncheon was going to start in ten minutes. If I was going to get back to the hall in time, I would have to hurry. I briefly thought about running through the bush and into the main gate of the school. But if anyone saw me coming in, they would know I'd been outside without permission. No, the only way back was through Elena's tunnel. So I went back over to the entrance, climbed down the first few stairs and pulled the door shut behind me, closing me off into the darkness of the secret passage.

Chapter 18

Finally, I climbed back through the panel and into the bathroom. I coughed lightly from the dust in the passageway and tried to pull the panel back across its runners. At first it squeaked along, but then it froze. I pulled one way, then pushed the other.

Jammed!

I looked around for something to help me close the panel, but there was nothing.

I knew I had a choice, then. I could either waste time trying to get this thing shut and miss Zoe's speech, or I could take Zoe her anklet and risk someone else finding the passage. After one last unsuccessful try, I decided I needed to get to Zoe.

I ran out of the bathroom and back down the stairs of the dormitory. I bundled out the front door, and sprinted across the lawn and back up the path, which wound through the school to the main courtyard. By the time I got to the fountain, I was panting heavily. I gulped in some air and kept running. I burst through the function hall doors, causing a few of the guests to startle.

"Slow down, you hoodlum!" Grace's Great-Aunt Clarice scolded as I ran past.

I didn't have time for Great-Aunt Clarice, so I kept jogging to the front of the room, where Zoe was pacing nervously. Mrs. Sinclair, the Headmistress, and Lauren, the School Captain, were trying to reassure her.

"It's OK, I've found it!" I exclaimed.

Mrs. Sinclair's eyes lit up. "See? I told you it would be somewhere obvious!"

Zoe's eyes widened and a huge smile spread across her face. She threw her arms around me. "Thank you, Ella. You really are a true best friend!"

Zoe undid the clasp and looped it over her ankle, then pulled her sock up over the top. She glanced at Mrs. Sinclair and Lauren. "So, am I in big trouble for wearing jewelry?"

Mrs. Sinclair smiled and looked at Lauren. "What jewelry? I didn't see any jewelry! Did you, Lauren?"

Lauren shook her head. "None at all!"

Zoe smiled widely.

"You've got this," I said, patting her arm.

Zoe's eyes were filled with a new confidence. She smiled, then stood up straight and stepped up to the microphone next to Lauren.

"Welcome to the Alumni Luncheon," Lauren said in a cool, confident voice. "I'm the School Captain, Lauren."

"And I," Zoe said, leaning into the microphone, "am a new Year 7 student at Eden College. My name is Zoe, and Lauren and I will be your hosts today."

Zoe then began to talk about her experience joining Eden College. Some of the guests had taken their seats, others remained standing. They all looked different, but they had one thing in common—they were all smiling and nodding as Zoe spoke clearly and proudly.

I slipped toward the back of the room, knowing I should be in the kitchen helping with the dishwashing.

"Back to it, Cinderella," I whispered to myself.

In the kitchen, everyone was busy getting the finger food ready for distribution. The Year 7 waitresses would take the sandwiches, canapés and dessert treats around to the guests in the breaks between the speeches and performances. It was up to the caterer's professional waitresses to keep the guests refreshed with tea, coffee and freshly squeezed juice, as they enjoyed the performances.

I slipped on my apron, which I had left on the countertop, and joined my friend Ruby at the sink.

"You dry, I'll wash?" she said, smiling.

I nodded.

"What did we do wrong to deserve a job like this?" she joked.

I took a metal bowl from her and spun it around in my hand as I wiped it dry with a tea towel. "Oh, I don't know," I said, thoughtfully. "I think it's OK being behind-the-scenes sometimes. My Nanna Kate always says it's the musicians in the pit that make the show."

"What do you mean?" Ruby asked.

"Whenever she takes us to the ballet or to a musical, she always makes us stay till the very last note is played. That's when they usually point to the musicians, who are hidden below the stage. She reckons they are the true heroes of the show."

Ruby smiled and nodded, understanding.

I could hear the rambunctious applause (that means very loud clapping and whooping) as Zoe finished up her speech in the adjoining room.

"And now we are going to have a soliloquy from one of our Drama students," Zoe said.

"Oh, this is Violet!" I squealed. "Let's go take a peek!"

Ruby and I snuck over to the kitchen door and peeked through its narrow rectangular window. I could see Violet taking the stage. She was dressed in a white dress and she pulled a large piece of cardboard up behind her, which was cut and painted to look like the top of a balcony. It had painted green ivy leaves crawling up the front and, when she stood behind it, it appeared as if she was standing on the little balcony, looking down below. She was doing a scene from Shakespeare's famous play *Romeo and Juliet*, and was playing the part of Juliet.

I was in awe of Violet as she spoke the words with such emotion and confidence. Even though the words in that play were antiquated (that means old and dusty), I felt like I really understood what was going on, just by the way she was saying the words.

My eyes darted around the room. I saw Eden Girls sitting with their relatives, either linking arms with them or holding their hands. I felt a sudden pang of homesickness in that moment—what I wouldn't give to have Mum or Nanna Kate standing there with me.

As I scanned the room, my eyes caught on something. It was like recognizing someone from the past, but not being quite able to pick how you knew them . . . someone from another life.

An old lady—very old—was sitting on a chair listening with her eyes closed. She had a smile on her weathered face and she was nodding as she absorbed the words of Violet's piece. She leaned on her cane with her trembling hands, and those hands, lined with the creases of time, had rings on each finger, all with beautiful stones in the center. She wore a flowered summer skirt with a white blouse, and, despite the heat, was wearing an embroidered cream cardigan. On her cardigan, I'd noticed something glisten as it caught the light. I looked once, then looked again.

It was something I recognized . . .

It was gold.

It was beautifully ornate.

I squinted. What was that familiar shape?

Could it be?

It was an Italian sparrow brooch.

Chapter 19

I reached into my school dress pocket and pulled out Elena's Italian sparrow brooch. It felt cold in my hands. I ran my fingers over the crevices on the wings. Then I squinted through the window again. Sure enough, the brooch the woman was wearing looked uncannily similar. But how could that be? Elena's father had made the brooch for his daughter—it wasn't from a popular jewelry store. This was one of a kind.

I waited until Violet's soliloquy was finished. The crowd applauded loudly as she took a bow. Then Zoe and Lauren stepped back up to the podium.

"Thank you, Violet," Lauren beamed. "Now, if everyone can please find their seat at the tables, our waitresses will be bringing around sandwiches and other lunchtime delights."

There was a loud scuffling as the standing ladies in the room moved with their younger relatives to find a seat. I saw Grace following behind her great-aunt as she hustled people out of her path with her walking stick.

The old woman with the brooch was already sitting at a table, but she turned inward, away from the podium. She looked around with a smile on her face, but she didn't seem to have anyone with her.

"Excuse me, please move. We need to get this food out," the catering manager scolded me. I was blocking the door to the function room.

"Oh, sorry," I stammered, jumping out of the way.

"Shouldn't you be over at the dishwashing station?" she asked me. "Quick sticks, get back to it!"

I wandered back to the sink with a million thoughts running through my head. Should I approach the old lady? Maybe she knew something about Elena's family and what had happened to them.

"Can you keep going here for a minute?" I asked Ruby, as she continued to scrub the plates. "I just need to get something."

Ruby nodded.

I took off my apron and straightened my dress, pulled up my socks and tightened my hair ribbon. Then I walked through the kitchen door and into the function room. Everyone was talking and laughing loudly. The Eden alumni ladies seemed to be having a wonderful time, telling stories of their youthful days in the school.

I walked slowly toward the old lady, not taking my eyes off her. But when I got to the front of the room where she was sitting, I realized I didn't know what to say. She looked up at me with deep brown eyes. Her olive skin was weathered and her hair was silvery. She smiled curiously at me.

"Excuse me," I stammered, "do you mind if I ask you something?"

"Please sit, *bambina*," she said in a warm voice, nodding to the chair next to her. "I have nobody here with me today, so I would very much like some company. What is your name?"

I smiled and pulled the chair out.

"My name is Ella. I was taken by your brooch," I said. "It's so . . . unique. I was wondering where you had gotten it from?"

She stroked her fingers over the brooch.

"It's beautiful, isn't it?" she said wistfully. "My father made it."

Her father? But that would mean . . .

Speechless, I reached into my pocket and pulled out the matching brooch. As I lifted it up, her eyes widened. Her mouth dropped open a little and she gasped.

"But . . . but, how?" she asked, reaching out to touch it. I passed it to her. "My father only made two. This one I am wearing belonged to my sister, who sadly passed away many years ago. My brooch I lost decades ago . . . Can it be?"

"So, you are . . . you are Elena?" I asked in a shaky voice.

"Why, yes! How did you know?"

I felt the world spinning around me. Everything had finally come together. But I still had so many questions.

"Elena!" I breathed. "I found your journal. It was hidden in the bell tower. I hope you don't mind that I read it—I found it all so intriguing!"

"Oh, the *bell tower*!" she exclaimed, clutching her hand to her chest. "My memory is not so good now. I knew I had hidden it in a wall, but I couldn't for the life of me remember where!" Elena spoke in an accent much the same as Zoe's Italian nonna.

"Yes! And your journal led me to . . ." I leaned in closer and whispered, "the secret tunnel. It's where I found your brooch!"

Elena leaned in and put her hands over mine. "So the tunnel does still exist!" she laughed. "My grandson dropped me here today and I made him come with me into the bushland earlier to try and find the entrance! I wanted to show him that my story was true. But we couldn't find it. He thought I was quite batty!"

That must have been who I had seen in the bush when I was looking for Zoe's anklet.

"But Elena, where did you go? Your journal ended so abruptly," I said.

Elena nodded. A wave of sadness washed over her face.

"Ella, there have been dark times in human history. Times which bring out the worst of human nature. And, sadly, war is one of those times."

"You wrote your journal during World War II," I said, remembering what I'd learned in the library.

"Indeed. And in that war, Italy and Australia were on different sides. I will tell you, *bambina*, the seed of suspicion in people's hearts can grow into a very dark thing. It can grow from doubt into unkindness and even, sometimes, into hate. It was a hard time for my family here. Girls in the school—lovely girls who were not bad people— were led to distrust people from nations on the other side of the war. People in the city stopped going to my father's jewelry shop. Then one day, someone smashed his store window. It was at that moment he admitted the war had divided us and decided to take us home to Italy, while he still could." Tears welled up in her eyes.

"I'm so sorry," I said, clasping her hands. "My best friend Zoe is Italian." I pointed to the front of the room where she was standing. "I can't imagine her being an outcast simply because of where she is from. It's so sad."

"It was not all so bad," she said, dabbing her eyes with a tissue, which she'd pulled from inside the cuff of her cardigan. "Moving home to Italy meant we were back with the rest of our family. When the war ended, I spent many a happy year there."

"So, what has brought you back?" I asked.

"Well, would you believe, it was when I was living in Italy that I fell in love with an Australian man. He had been in the war as a soldier—just a young boy of 18 at the time. He loved it so much over there that he stayed when the war ended. We met when I was a grown adult and we fell in love and married in my uncle's vineyard."

I smiled.

"And then, in time, we decided to move back to Australia. In many ways, it was like coming home again. While a piece of my heart will always be in Italy, Australia is my home, too."

"How did it come to be that you are here at the Alumni Luncheon?" I asked. "Do you have family at Eden?"

"No, I don't," she said, shaking her head. "But I have been invited today because I am the oldest living Eden Girl. I am 95 years old! Can you believe that? I can't. Inside, I still feel like the same little girl who spent her days in the bushland by the tunnel. Yet here I am—an old lady."

"My Nanna Kate says that the body ages, but as long as your soul still sings, your heart will not grow old," I said.

Elena nodded. "And even though my days at Eden were tainted with sadness, I did love this place—the teaching, the Australian bush."

My heart swelled in my chest. I couldn't believe it. I had found Elena. And I had finally heard the end of her story. It all made sense now—if she had to leave quickly during the war, that was why she wasn't in any records at Eden College. She had already left by the time they had taken the photographs for her year group. She had been here such a short time that she had existed in the school without ever leaving a trace. Like a ghost.

"Ella, shouldn't you be in the kitchen?" a voice said behind me.

I turned and saw Saskia walking back toward her table, which was filled with all her alumni relatives.

"Oh," I said, gathering myself.

"No!" Elena said, grasping my arm before I could stand. "She is with *me*."

Saskia shook her head, confused, but walked off to her table.

I smiled at Elena.

"She's got lots of Eden relatives," I said, nodding in Saskia's direction. "It's like she's Eden royalty. I don't have anyone here, so I really should be in the kitchen."

Elena smiled with her kind eyes. "It's not who your relatives are that makes you special, you know." Elena was still holding the brooch I had given to her. She gently lifted her hands and opened the clasp on the back. Then she reached out and pinned it to my uniform.

"For you, my friend, Ella," she whispered.

"Thank you, Elena," I smiled, astonished at her generosity. "You know, I was in your secret passage just today! I used it to help my friend Zoe," I said, pointing up to the lectern again. "She lost something very precious in the bush, so I used your tunnel to find it."

"That was very brave, *bambina*," Elena said. "You could have been in trouble. But you did it for your friend?"

I nodded.

"You have a good heart," she said, squeezing my arm.

The microphone made a light squeal as Zoe and Lauren stepped back up to the podium. Zoe cleared her throat and began to speak. "It is my great honor to introduce our next guest to you. This guest is our oldest living Eden alumni. Please welcome Ms. Elena Partridge."

I looked at Elena in surprise. I hadn't expected that she would be giving a speech today. She strained as she tried to stand, so I jumped up and helped her. I supported her arm and walked her up to the podium, then pulled the microphone down to her level, as she leaned on her cane.

She nodded her thanks as I sat back down in my seat.

"It is a great honor to be here today," she said in her quiet crackly voice. "I don't have a lot to say—which is probably a relief to many of you, who do not wish to listen to the ramblings of an old lady."

Everyone in the room laughed politely.

"It's a curious thing to come back within the walls of Eden College. When I was here as a girl, it was a troubled time. It was during the war, and, as many of you know, war breeds darkness, and the softest of hearts can turn to stone. But it's also a great pleasure to be here today. I have been reminded that while I was here a long time ago, there are still strands that connect us all—strong cords that transcend history and time. And the strongest of those is something that was very precious *then* and is very precious *now*. And that is *friendship*. It is my honor to introduce to you my very special friend, Ella. She is a true Eden Girl because she is strong and brave and kind."

My heart leapt in my chest as Elena said my name. She beckoned me up to stand by her side at the podium. The room applauded for Elena as she raised her glass to everyone in the room.

I looked around and saw Saskia sitting at her table in utter shock. Even though she was there with all her relatives, it was me who was standing up at the podium with Eden's most special guest.

Maybe Saskia *was* wrong about what made someone special at Eden College. Maybe it had nothing to do with who you were related to. Maybe, just maybe, it had more to do with the friendships you made. And the size of your heart.

Chapter 20

✕ −

From: <u>Ella</u>

Sent: Tuesday, 6:05 PM

To: <u>Olivia</u>

Subject: Elena at Eden

Hi Olivia!

I'm still spinning out about finding Elena yesterday. Did you tell Mum and Dad about it after I spoke to you on the phone?

Elena even came back to the school today! Her grandson

brought her in and I was able to give her back her journal and do a big interview with her, all about life at Eden during the war.

It's SUCH an interesting article and I can't wait to publish it in *Eden Press*. I showed Ivy my draft and she loved it so much she made me show it to Mrs. Sinclair and Monty. Mrs. Sinclair cried when she read it, and I think I even caught Monty dabbing her eye with a tissue!

The only bad thing that happened was that Monty found the secret passageway. And Grace, Zoe and Violet never even got to see it! I couldn't get the panel to shut after I found Zoe's anklet, and it was discovered. Turns out that the passageway was built in World War I as an emergency escape route. But everybody kind of forgot about it after the dorm was renovated sometime in the 1960s.

Of course, I did get into a bit of trouble for using it without permission. I had to own up—Monty said she knew somebody had opened it and the guilty party had better come forward. But Mrs. Sinclair said I wasn't really in big trouble—she said if she had found a secret passage, she would have explored it, too! But in the future, if I am ever to find any other "surprise structural anomalies" at the school, I have to report them immediately.

I wasn't punished, but the sad part of the story is that they've closed up the access to the passageway. Some builders came and said it "lacked structural integrity," which is just a fancy way of saying it wasn't safe and could fall down. They had no choice but to close it up for good.

So that's the end of my secret adventures in there! Although you never know . . . this place is just full of surprises. Who knows what I might discover next time?

Miss you.

Love, Ella

xx

About the Author

Ever since she learned to hold a pen, Laura Sieveking has loved creating stories. She remembers hiding in her room as a six-year-old, writing a series of books about an unlikely friendship between a princess and a bear.

As an adult, Laura has spent the vast majority of her career working in publishing as an editor. After several years, she decided to put down her red pen and open up her laptop to create books of her own.

Laura's books revolve around all the things she loved as a child—friendships, sports and a little bit of magic. She has written series for early independent readers and middle grade fiction.

She lives in Sydney, Australia, with her husband and two children, and her fluffy dog who looks like a teddy bear.

ELLA AT EDEN

Read all the Ella at Eden adventures:

New Girl
The Secret Journal